$LIM DOUG
BILLIONAIRE

MADHU SOLANKI

ARCHWAY
PUBLISHING

Archway Publishing books may be ordered through booksellers or by contacting:

Archway Publishing
1663 Liberty Drive
Bloomington, IN 47403
www.archwaypublishing.com
844-669-3957

ISBN: 978-1-6657-1554-6 (sc)
ISBN: 978-1-6657-1555-3 (e)

Library of Congress Control Number: 2021923724

Print information available on the last page.

Archway Publishing rev. date: 12/23/2021

CONTENTS

ACKNOWLEDGMENTS

I thank my friends and colleagues, each noble human I came across in my life, my parents, my siblings, my teachers, authors, preachers, and neighbors for planting the seed that led to the creation of this book.

Special thanks are due to the entire Archway Publishing staff, starting from the first phone call. I should thank the cover designer and each printing staff member all the way through marketing.

—Madhu Solanki

CHAPTER 1
JACKPOT

It was nighttime. A live TV show was being taped in the town of Luckville in the country of Prosperia. The commercial break was over, and the show continued.

"Welcome back to your favorite show, *Wild Guess, Right Answer*. Today is the final day for five million dollars to be given out," the moderator said.

He looked at the contestant and said, "So, Kamal, are you ready? Go again. If your answer is correct, you carry home five million dollars!"

Kamal looked at the globe displayed in the monitor.

"How old is Mother Earth, our home? Is it two thousand twenty years old, fourteen million years old, four million years old, or more?" the moderator asked.

"I don't know. Let me think," Kamal said. He scratched his head and looked around and up. He held his face with both hands and stroked his chin.

Suddenly, he said, "I know I have read it somewhere. Uh … uh. Four point fifty- five billion years?"

The bell tinged *yes*.

"You are right! Congratulations! You just became a millionaire five times," the moderator said.

Confetti dropped from the ceiling, and victory music played. The audience exploded with joy, giving him a lengthy applause.

The moderator continued, "Ladies and gentlemen, meet our new millionaire, Kamal Din."

Kamal's family—his wife, Rubina, and children, Douglas and Sheena—rushed to the stage.

The moderator said, "Kamal, you won a lot of money. What are you going to do with it?"

"I don't know yet. I am thinking. I am thinking. Let it sink in first. Maybe I will make more money—more and more," Kamal answered.

"Will you introduce your family please?" the moderator asked.

Kamal obliged. "This is my dear wife, Rubina. And here are my children, Douglas and Sheena."

"Hey, big guy," the moderator said to Douglas. "Are you happy? Your dad just won five million dollars."

"Yeah," Douglas said.

Kamal's family sneaked out to the parking lot through the back door.

"Kamal … hey, Kamal!" a guy shouted when they came out. Kamal hurried to leave, but the man followed him.

The guy said again, "Hey, you won, so now you're not looking at us. You big shot."

A second wise guy stepped forward. "Yo, your dad owed my daddy money. Give it to me."

Now, a moderately dressed skinny gentleman wearing a T-shirt marked "People's Charity" stepped in front. He had his bag hanging on his shoulder. He walked up and gave Kamal a pamphlet.

"Sir, we are from People's Charity. Remember our organization please. God bless you," the man said.

The guy left, but the crowd kept on surrounding the Din family. They ran and somehow managed to reach their car.

The next morning, curious people crowded Kamal's home street. Even the local television crew was present.

Outside Kamal's home, a TV reporter lady walked toward the front door.

The reporter talked to the studio anchorman while looking at the camera. "Ladies and gentlemen, we are in front of a new multimillionaire's home."

"Debra, can you tell us more about him?" the anchorman asked.

"Well, Jim, Kamal Din and his family don't want to give any interviews; however, people say that he works for a town culinary enterprise."

"In what capacity?"Asked the anchorman.

"That is not clear. Some say he is a manager of a big corporation cafeteria. Back to you, Jim."

Kamal's mother, Jane, had also arrived and started cooking Kamal's favorite dish to celebrate his victory. Her curious grandchildren also joined her in the kitchen.

"What are you cooking, Grandma Jane?"

"Your dad won, so today I am going cook his favorite dish."

Douglas stepped in and touched the recipe book.

"Wow, how big is it? Grandma, I always love your delicious recipes. Will you teach me how to cook?" He asked.

Visitors started coming in and leaving. Kamal ran around to receive them while answering incoming phone calls.

Kamal answered the phone. "Yes, of course I remember you. Thanks for the compliments," he said.

Then the doorbell rang, and Kamal opened the door to find a stranger.

"Hello, Kamal, my friend. Remember me?"

"No."

"Congratulations."

The stranger handed him a bouquet of flowers and continued, "Your dad and my dad grew up in the same neighborhood. They promised to help each other in times of need."

He handed Kamal a note and said, "And here is my address."

Kamal thanked the guy. When he glanced at the crowd outside, they became elated and shouted at him.

"Hey!"

A police car arrived with flashing lights. A police officer started speaking.

"Break it up. Nothing to see; it's illegal to gather here. Go home."

The crowd moved away, and the police left. Then the crowd came back and made noise. Kamal shut the door. The phone rang. Kamal ran. His wife, Rubina, tried to stop him.

"Listen, this thing is getting out of hand. It's crazy. We have to do something."

Kamal turned around, walked to the window, and peeked outside by slightly moving the curtain.

"My God," he mumbled. "People are unbelievable."

He went back inside and yelled, "Look! More people. We can't live like this any longer."

"What are we going to do now?" Rubina said.

"We will have to move," Kamal replied.

"Let's move to the other side of town into the elite neighborhood."

"No, I'm thinking of a better place."

"Where?"

"We will leave the country. Go abroad, far, far away where nobody will bother us."

"Which country?"

"Let's go to the USA, where there is Disneyland, Hollywood, and Las Vegas. And we will start our own business. The United States of America—that's the place to be."

The wall TV showed beautiful Californian scenery. Planes were taking off. Some landed. Modern cars were running on the winding highway.

Kamal sat down thinking.

"Yeah, let's go to the USA," Rubina added. "Start our own business. Invest our money. Good idea."

America

The Din family arrived at the Los Angeles airport. Passengers' were coming out of the immigration area. The family waited to pick up their luggage at the carousel. Foursomes came up on an escalator. Douglas and Sheena grew playful.

Their limo drove away under a green highway sign that read 405N. After maneuvering through traffic, the Din family arrived in front of their quiet suburban home. For a while, they stayed inside the car and looked at their house in amazement.

The kids flung open the doors, jumped out, threw their shoulder bags on the ground, and ran into the rear of the house, where they started playing on the slide and swing.

A chubby, middle-aged real estate agent, wearing a cowboy hat and holding a cigar in his mouth, soon arrived to meet with Kamal and Rubina.

"Congratulations, folks. Welcome to your new home. This is a great neighborhood. It has the best schools, there's no crime, and it's a peaceful place." He shook Kamal's hand and gave him the keys. Kamal dugout a white envelope and handed it to the agent.

"Here is your money," Kamal said.

The agent half-opened the envelope, looked inside, and put the money away in his briefcase. He started walking around the house. Kamal and Rubina followed.

They entered a huge backyard and continued past a blue swimming pool. The kids were already playing there.

Douglas shouted, "Dad, look at our barbecue grill! I am going to cook."

"Mom, this table is mine, and this is my s-s-special seat," Sheena added.

$ $ $

The next day, Kamal and Rubina went to the real estate office.

Kamal announced while entering, "I called you about buying a business."

The agent stepped forward and said, "Oh yes. Sit down. How do you like your new home?"

"Wonderful," Rubina said.

The agent gave Kamal some forms to fill out. Then he went inside and came back out with a thick, old-fashioned file. He started turning pages.

"I think we have a few places downtown you would be interested in. Let's go," he said.

The agent donned his coat, put his hat on, and drove off with the couple. They went through LA's streets and proceeded toward downtown. The car entered a low-income neighborhood. They stopped at a broken-down coffee shop. There was a graffiti logo on the door. The graffiti-filled wall announced the presence of gangs. Names such as Bay Boy, the Sneak, and Leon King were crudely painted on the wall.

The agent searched for the keys and opened the squeaky door. They all waved away the stinky smell with their hands.

Frightened rats ran away. Then the couple and agent went further to the next place.

They talked to the seller.

"Gentlemen, it is a nice property," the big-mouth seller said.

"Why are you selling it?" Kamal asked.

"We're moving to Las Vegas."

"Wow. Las Vegas. That's where the money is, isn't it? How is your business here?"

"You make a pretty good profit in the season."

"Oh, it is seasonal. No, no, no, not that type of business."

Kamal whispered something in the agent's ear, and they walked out.

"The last one is on the northwestern hill area. It's a posh location. It's always the location, location, location," the agent raved.

"I'm dreaming of a five-star restaurant. Customers, customers, customers," Kamal answered.

The agent gave him an impish smile.

"A good location with good people, you see. Because I want to make a big profit—like billions of dollars," Kamal added.

The agent turned around and smiled sarcastically. "OK, guys, let's go to see the last one," he declared.

All three got into the car and drove farther on. Finally, they arrived at an amazing, hilly dream location.

"Wow, wow! This is it. Why didn't you show us this in the first place?" Kamal asked.

They walked inside. Kamal and Rubina checked out everything. Both were impressed and satisfied. Rubina moved closer to Kamal.

"Now don't get excited. Poker face, poker face. He won't reduce the price," she whispered in Kamal's ear.

"If you like it, come to the office tomorrow. We'll work it out. I will prepare the paperwork for you to sign, "The agent said.

The next day, the Din family came back to the office. The kids, playing with their digital game devices, followed their parents. Kamal filled out some papers. The agent went inside the boss's office and returned with the boss, who was a well-dressed and somewhat chubby guy. He shook hands with Kamal and then returned to his office.

The agent explained to Kamal and Rubina what was written on the document. They listened to the agent carefully while bending over the table.

"Both of you sign here, here, and here. Initial all the boxes," the agent requested and left.

After signing, excited, Kamal declared, "I can make a billion dollars now."

The jealous agent overheard that. He came back in and said, "Can you even spell a billion. It is not just by replacing m with b."

"I know it is three zeros more," Kamal replied.

Douglas and Sheena were listening. They stopped playing, approached the table, and peeked at the papers.

The agent said, "Kids, a billion is one thousand million, not by adding three zeros more, never mind."

"A fortuneteller has told me that we will be billionaires one day," Kamal explained.

"Oh, sure. Why not? Keep dreaming," the agent replied.

Rubina quickly interjected, "Don't boast, suppose something goes wrong, and you can't be successful."

Kamal blurted out louder, "If not me, my children will make billions."

Both kids walked closer to the agent saying, "Yeahhhh …"

"That, I believe, "the agent said.

CHAPTER 2

FAST LIFE

Kamal and Rubina went shopping to a restaurant supply warehouse. Little Douglas followed them, pushing a cart. Kamal filled the cart to the brim and continued piling on more.

"What are you doing?" Rubina questioned.

"Buying stuff."

"Please don't buy things you don't need. No money will be left."

"Yeah, Dad," Douglas agreed.

"You know your dad gets carried away," Rubina told Douglas.

"What do you mean?" Kamal asked.

"I think you should also involve your chefs, Armando, Emile, Chao, and Monteiro," Rubina replied.

"Why?"

"Chefs know the best."

"How come?" Douglas inquired.

"Chefs are seasoned," Rubina explained. She stepped closer to Kamal. "Real business runs from bottom to top."

Douglas interrupted. "Dad, Italian restaurants have huge ovens. Indians need a tandoor, and Chinese people want a wok, you know."

"And what do Americans need?" Rubina interjected.

"Grills!" Father and son shouted together.

Douglas returned and said, "By the way, it is not 'walk,' and it is pronounced 'woke.' Yes, I saw it on TV."

"A smart kid. Right on, my baby," Rubina approved.

"Yes, boss, you could be my right-hand man." Kamal saluted him.

They filled up two carts with pots, pans, and some ingredients. Then they paid and walked out of the store.

When they returned to the restaurant, the workers were applying the finishing touches to their newly purchased Super Imperial Cuisine building, a rapid, last-minute refurbishing. A band was playing near the entrance of Kamal's new restaurant's "GRAND OPENING" sign. Kamal proudly stood near the door.

In the evening, elegantly dressed Rubina and the children arrived. They stepped inside. Little Sheena started helping Rubina straighten the bright-white tablecloths. Curious, Douglas walked right into the kitchen and looked at the well-dressed chefs. Sheena followed him.

Douglas talked to Chef Monteiro. "Hi, my name is Douglas. May I help you, sirs?"

"Help? What kind of help you can give, little man?"

"I can cut onions and potatoes. And, oh, I can make coffee, tea, and all kinds of funky drinks like my grandma."

"Really?" Monteiro wondered.

"And I can make a billion-dollar profit."

"Do you know what it looks like?"

Douglas turned to his sister. "You know, sis, a billion has only three zeros more than a million."

Sheena raised her left hand wide open. She counted out a couple of fingers and said, "Yeah."

Standing on a box, Douglas cracked some eggs to make an omelet. A man dressed in a waiter's uniform dashed in.

"Hey, everybody, customers have started arriving."

People formed a big line in front. The maître d' led them to their respective tables and gave each a fancy menu card.

Plants and flower pots added to the atmosphere inside. The Super Imperial Cuisine's parking lot was filling up fast. The restaurant got busy.

Chefs Monteiro, Armando, Chao, and Emile hopped into action. They had nice name tags over their bright-white uniforms. Their cooking stations were marked Chinese, Mexican, Italian, and American. There was a list of items from tea to tacos on the shelves.

Little Sheena welcomed patrons with an exaggerated bow and went to each table to give them extra menu cards. Kamal came and took the remaining cards away from her.

"Good job, young lady. Now relax and watch," Dad told his daughter.

Elegantly dressed people arrived, ate, and left. Waiters ran around, carrying trays of fancy food in their raised palms.

A customer walked up to Kamal's cashier counter after finishing his meal.

"Congratulations, mister, for starting a new business. About time. We need a good restaurant in this community."

Many compliments like this came in.

$ $ $

It was another busy day at the Super Imperial Cuisine. People were lining up in the front. Soft music was playing. The restaurant soon filled up.

Kamal was sitting at the cashier counter, counting money. In his hands, he held a bundle of hundred-dollar bills, which he proudly shuffled like a pack of cards.

A stocky guy donning a cowboy hat with a cigar in his mouth had just finished his meal. He stopped to pay the bill.

The guy looked at the bundle of dollars in Kamal's hands.

"Nice dough, man. You should visit Las Vegas one day."

"Really?" Kamal responded.

"I have my business over there. There is glitz, glamour, and the high life. Good luck with your new business."

The guy then left.

The next weekend day, Kamal was all dressed up and ready to go with his travel bag. He talked to Rubina from the kitchen door.

"Honey, you'll have to manage restaurant this weekend."

"Where are you going?" a surprised Rubina questioned.

"Business, honey, business. There is a lot of money in Las Vegas."

"Do you have to? You think only money can buy happiness."

"Well, money buys things that make you happy. And you want to be happy, don't you?"

"Don't lose your mind gambling. Las Vegas is called Sin City, you know."

"I'll help Mom," Douglas interrupted.

Kamal left quietly to adventure in Las Vegas.

$ $ $

Kamal entered a posh casino sporting his beard. He checked out all the food stalls and became overwhelmed while hearing the tinkling sound of slot machines.

He walked further on, went to a craps table, and watched people playing, drinking, and smoking. He smiled when winners collected handfuls of chips.

"Hey, come on! Sit down. Have fun!" one player invited Kamal.

He sat down and bought some chips. The counter man sent the money through his vacuum system.

Kamal lost his first game. Then he won a few.

"Waiter, a round of beer for everyone on me!" Kamal ordered.

His fellow players seemed impressed.

A couple of hookers came and stood next to him, applauding. He felt proud. Kamal was on a roll. He kept on playing and lost all his chips. He walked out to the parking lot.

$ $ $

The next day in the casino, the floor traffic was busy. Well-dressed, elite people were sitting at a card table playing poker. Many of them were smoking while holding their cocktail glasses. Kamal took a big puff on his cigar.

"Man, I love weekends. This sure is a great place," Kamal declared, while coughing, in front of busy gamblers.

"Come on down, man! Have fun!" a fellow gambler said to Kamal.

"I want to play blackjack; I have heard it's easy. I want to learn how to win and make millions," he said.

"Millions? Then join us. You need to play poker, man. Make millions, guy. Blackjack is for kids."

Reluctantly, Kamal sat and watched. He was surprised when the dealer dealt him his cards.

"Yeah, yeah, your turn. Have you ever tried this?" A fellow gambler proposed.

"No …"

"Listen, blackjack is fast. Poker is slow but intelligent. You have got the whole night. Watch and learn," another gambler said.

"All right, looks like today is my lucky day. Baby wants a new pair of shoes!" He joined in.

"That's for a high-roller," the first gambler explained.

They let him win the first time.

"Drinks for everyone, please," Kamal asked a passing bar girl.

The game continued. Kamal lost this game but played more and more. He lost everything and got bored. He threw down his cards, stood up, and left.

"Oh God, I lost all my chips." He coughed, keeping his fist on his mouth.

He went to a cashier's window, talked to him, and argued with him. His hand gestures showed that he was upset. He walked back.

Kamal challenged his fellow players, "See you guys next week. I am warning you, next week will be tough for you."

A fellow player made an offer, "Hey, you want some cash to go back? Seriously."

"No, thanks, I have a return ticket," he said.

Kamal walked toward the exit. He noticed "Breaking news" alert on the wall TV.

The TV anchorman announced, "Breaking news. Vicious wildfires have broken out in the northwest hills of Los Angeles. The fire advances further. People and businesses are being evacuated from the area."

Kamal came running back to the table. He talked to his game buddies.

"Did you see that?"

He pointed at a wall TV. The Santa Ana winds were blowing hard. Tree trunks were brushing against each other. Limbs were falling; they could hear the crackling sound of burning dry wood. Bright-orange flames were creating a river of dark clouds far up in the sky. Smoke was blowing toward the city. The hill looked like well-done barbecue charcoal.

"The cause of the fire is not known yet. A wet spring had grown plenty of greenery. The hot dry summer has created plentiful of fuel of dry grass and wood, material ready to burn," the anchorman continued.

A picture of an awfully red-hot mountain was visible on the TV.

"Rangers are not sure whether it is manmade or natural. It could be from a brush fire or from lightning. Unfortunately, there is no rain. People are praying for rain, a lot of rain," the anchorman added.

The TV showed pictures of burning houses and businesses. The debris was flying in the air.

"Whether it started from a campfire or an unattended barbecue grill, only time will tell," the anchorman added.

"Maybe some moron threw a live cigar butt," Kamal mumbled.

Kamal hurriedly returned home.

$ $ $

When the rain stopped, the governor visited the area in his helicopter. The smoke was disappearing. A series of fire department vehicles were lined up on a country road. Exhausted people were trying to go past the National Guard. A guard stopped Kamal.

"My restaurant is there, man."

"Can't go in."

He returned home.

Kamal started watching the TV news.

"A lot of damage is evident all over the area. It will take days to recover," the anchorman said.

Kamal decided to rebuild the restaurant. Construction workers were soon busy doing their jobs, dressed in their work clothes while carrying their gear. They went in and out of the building.

Kamal watched the work being done. Carpenters hammered some planks into the wall. Painters painted. Slowly, the building came alive. Workers worked all around the building. Kamal appeared satisfied. The driveway and the parking lot were paved and white tracks were drawn.

An "OPEN" sign invited Super Imperial Cuisine customers in. Only a couple of tables were filled. A customer got up to pay the bill.

"Good food. Why is no one here?" a customer inquired of Kamal after finishing his meal.

"We were closed for more than a month. You know the fire. People don't know yet that we are open," Kamal answered while coughing.

The phone rang while Kamal was sitting and checking a bundle of bills at home.

"Mr. Kamal, this is North South Insurance Company. I have bad news for you," the caller said.

"What?" Kamal responded.

"Your insurance company does not cover a complete replacement of the roof."

The guy hung up. Depressed, Kamal sat alone.

A second caller rang. "Hey, Kamal, we need the money."

"Brother, be patient. Think of my business. The fire has totally barbecued my restaurant. I have to start from scratch. Understand?" Kamal replied while coughing.

"I don't care about your business. Pay me before you run away."

$ $ $

It was nighttime in Kamal's home. Kamal was relaxing on his couch, reading a newspaper. Rubina was working on a corner desk with a pile of papers.

Rubina complained in her cracking voice, "Where are we going to get this money from? I have to pay all these bills, lots of bills, both home and business expenses."

One by one, she opened the envelopes and then stared at the thick bundle of bills in her hands.

"I don't know what's happening to all the money we make. Tell me what you do in Las Vegas," Rubina inquired.

"Business, honey, business. I have to see my friends. Business meetings, you know," Kamal answered and coughed, keeping his hand on his mouth.

"And then?"

"Look, I work very hard here. I need some entertainment, too, for a change. Have to relax sometimes!" Kamal yelled.

Embarrassed and scared, the children listened, hiding behind the door.

"We still have to pay your cardiologist's bill, remember?" Rubina added.

"So?"

"When is your next appointment? God, he can't even keep up with doctor's appointments."

"I know sometime next month."

"And you have started smoking big-shot cigars."

"I can quit."

"What happened to the money we brought to this country after winning?"

"What money?" Kamal asked.

"And you want to be a billionaire. Huh."

"What are you talking about? So I made a boo-boo, okay?"

"You'll die early this way. Wake up! Think about your children at least."

Feeling guilty, Kamal became angry. He quickly put his jacket and hat on and left home. His car made a loud screeching sound as he pulled out of the driveway.

CHAPTER 3
TOUGH TIME

Kamal entered George's Bar. Inside, he leaned forward, put money on the counter, and ordered his favorite drink.

"Scotch on the rocks," he said.

Then he picked up his drink and sat in the corner thinking. He coughed often. Drink half finished, he held a cigar in his left hand. He coughed again and threw his cigar into the ashtray. Shaking, he put his left hand on his chest.

"Oh, no!" He screamed.

Kamal collapsed. His glass fell on the floor and rolled down toward the wall. He passed out.

$ $ $

At home, Rubina received the phone call.

"What? What happened?" Rubina asked.

"Ambulance was just called," the caller said.

Rubina screamed, "Oh my God! Send him directly to the Deep Valley Hospital, please."

$ $ $

Sirens shrieking, the ambulance arrived in front of the emergency entrance of Deep Valley Hospital. The flashing lights brightened the surroundings. The siren sounds echoed, announcing the arrival of a serious patient.

Technicians pulled the stretcher out. Kamal lay unconscious, breathing with oxygen tubes. He looked sweaty and pale.

The ER staff met him halfway with their machines and gadgets. Nurses checked his vital signs. New IV and oxygen tubes were connected.

The staff took their patient inside and drew the curtains.

"Dr. Joseph Smith, code blue, an announcement came over the speakers.

A group of doctors came rushing and checked everything out again.

$ $ $

Confused, Rubina arrived at ER. She looked from a distance and asked a technician.

"Is he Kamal?"

"Yes. And who are you?" the technician asked.

"I am his wife. Is he all right? What happened?"

She wanted to go inside. She tried to get in, but the technician stopped her with his outstretched hands.

"You can't go inside."

"But I am his wife," Rubina argued.

She waited on the bench outside. A middle-aged doctor wearing a white coat and a stethoscope came out.

"It appears to be a massive heart attack. His alcohol level is way over the limit. Come with me."

The doctor walked inside the room. Emotional, Rubina followed him, shaking. She watched Kamal closely as he lay in his bed. She tried to pat him.

After a big cough and a deep breath, Kamal exhaled his last. The nurse checked his pulse and ran out. She returned with the doctor, who checked Kamal again with the stethoscope. He talked to the nurse quietly. She covered the body with a white sheet. The doctor walked away, keeping his head down.

Rubina screamed and ran toward the wall. She wept. The nurse took her to the side. Everything turned somber.

The next day, Kamal's burial ceremony was held at North Side Cemetery. Freshly created, the grave was fully covered with beautiful floral garlands. When the crowd started leaving and people began walking to their respective cars, two lonely kids ran back to the grave. They stood together, knelt, and mumbled something. Then they got up and turned around. They were Kamal's young children, Douglas and Sheena. Both ran back.

$ $ $

A few days later, the somber Din family was sitting quietly at home in their living room, trying to make sense of their situation. The kids were sad and did not understand what was happening. Rubina was holding a bundle of bills in her hand.

Sheena cuddled with her mom.

Rubina cleared her throat and began, "Kids, I want you to understand that we don't have a good income now. We can't afford to pay all these bills." She was trying to explain their reality to the children.

"But why did it happen to Dad?" Sheena inquired.

"We always prepare for these kinds of things in life, but we never know how it feels until it actually happens."

Rubina stopped and tried to think. She continued, "Children, we can't live here anymore. It's too expensive. We will have to move."

"But why?" Sheena argued.

"Things change from time to time. Sometimes, it is day, sometimes night," Rubina explained.

"So where are we moving to?" The kids asked.

"Wherever it is peaceful and cheaper. We have to sell everything and move upstate."

"But where, Mom? I will miss Kelly, Leah, Debbie, and all my friends, you know," Sheena pleaded.

"Whenever we have to move, think we are moving forward," Rubina replied.

Sheena began sobbing.

"Lenders have put a lien on our house to collect their money. That's why there is a for-sale sign outside," Rubina explained.

Sheena lifted her head and sniffed. As she wiped her face, she asked, "What is a lien?"

"You wouldn't understand, baby," Rubina replied with a lump in her throat.

Rubina sobbed a bit, and a couple of tears ran down her cheek. Douglas watched the whole thing. He got up, picked up a box, and gave his mom a tissue.

Douglas held out a book and declared, "The dictionary says a lien means a legal right to collect money … blah, blah, blah."

"*What*?" Sheena wondered aloud.

"Lenders file a claim to recover their money when the house or property is sold. Loan shark," Douglas added.

Rubina interrupted, "And when they legally issue an order to do so, it is called a lien." She stopped Douglas from continuing with her wide eyes and a gesture and said, "I recently found out your dad had mortgaged our restaurant to get loans."

"What is mortgage?"Sheena asked.

"The payment. If we don't pay the bank loan installment, return the borrowed money in time, they will foreclose on the property, and somebody will grab it cheaply," Rubina said.

She looked at Sheena and stroked her hair, uttering, "Now don't ask me what *foreclose* is."

She shifted her gaze to Douglas and said, "After a cheap sale, the seller has to pay the lender what he owes. You get only the leftover peanuts."

She paused.

"Foreclosure is not something you shut down four times. Understand? In short, the restaurant does not belong to us. So much for making billions and billions," Rubina continued.

Sheena insisted, "But it is our restaurant."

"It does not work that way. It belongs to the bank."

"Then what?"

"Nothing in this world is ours. Everything is temporary."

Both kids stared at her helplessly.

Douglas asserted, "Okay, Ma, don't worry. We're with you, whatever you decide."

He patted his mom's back. Sheena tightly hugged her and sobbed.

One cloudy day, the word "sold "overlapped the for-sale sign in front of the Din family home.

The front porch of the house was filled with packed belongings. Used cardboard boxes were filled and taped all around. Somewhat dark and dented pots and pans were tied together at the handles.

Some exercise gadgets and equipment were also lying on the ground. Rubina got on the phone as she stood on the sidewalk.

"Hey, discount transport company."

"What do you want?"the dispatcher replied.

"Gentlemen, it is time to go. Where are you? Look, it is the first of August. We are supposed to go."

"Your order was canceled," the dispatcher declared.

"What? Why? What are you talking about? I have paid the deposit."

"I can't find your deposit."

"I paid cash in person last week. I have a receipt."

"Lady, we have to fill bigger orders first."

The dispatcher's phone buzzed off with a sinister sound.

"Oh my God! What am I going to do now?" Rubina cried.

A posh car appeared in front of the house. It was the same selling agent, wearing his cowboy hat and holding a cigar in his mouth. He stepped out and walked up to her.

The agent demanded loudly, "What's going on, guys? You're still here? You were supposed to be gone."

He walked back and spoke to the people in the second car. They came out and started taking boxes away from the premises.

Somberly, Douglas was standing in the corner. His sister, Sheena, started crying as she held her mom's dress. She was carrying her beloved white bunny in her right hand.

The agent demanded, "Come on, people. Hurry up."

"Sir, we are moving. The truck did not arrive."

The agent said again, "Whatever, move your crummy junk from my property. Come on! Move it! Quick. It's over, millionaires."

The agent kicked a box. Douglas's eyes widened with anger. He ran and started moving boxes. He came back.

Douglas was mad. He whispered, "Stupid. Idiot. What does he mean?"

Rubina slapped him softly on his shoulder.

"No. We don't talk like that. We are not his type, young man."

"Sorry," Douglas apologized.

A huge rumble of thunder in the sky was threatening. It started raining. Rubina and the kids were waiting under a tree, soaking wet.

The agent shouted at Rubina from a distance, "Hey, what happened?"

"Gentleman, just because we are orphaned does not mean you have to abuse us."

"Hurry up! I have seen a lot like you. This is all my property. What do you have?"

Rubina said quickly, "Let me tell you something. I am not poor. Okay."

She put both her hands on her children's shoulders and said, "This is my wealth."

The family started moving stuff from the edge of the sidewalk. The rain began again. They went aside under a garage roof shed.

While they were waiting in the rain, Rubina called another moving company.

Rubina yelled, "Where is the new company now? It is time already."

A rundown truck came in. A long-haired, bearded, and tattooed young driver came out, saying, "You have to pay the deposit up front."

"Look, I already paid money to the other guy. They never came," she explained and paid.

It was time to load the stuff. Rubina looked at the driver.

"Don't look at me. I just do the driving. Not lifting."

Rubina took out her purse and gave him some more money.

The whole family helped the driver to load the goods. Rubina sat in front. The kids were between her and the driver. Sheena was holding her bunny in her lap.

The truck took off, making a loud exhaust sound, and drove down a winding middle California highway. It passed through hills and valleys. Bouncing and rattling, the truck proceeded onto the highway.

The truck stopped halfway there.

The driver looked at Rubina. "Ma'am, we don't have much fuel left."

"Didn't you check it before coming?"

"This was an emergency job, remember?"

"What do you want me to do? I gave you the money, didn't I?"

"That's the company's money."

Rubina reached for her purse again and gave him the money. The driver got down at a service station.

"Sucker," said Douglas and quickly uttered, "Sorry."

They filled up the gas tank. The driver came back and gave Rubina the receipt. They moved ahead. The truck went on and on through the hills and valleys on the winding highway for a long time. By and by, jumping and bouncing, the noisy truck arrived in a small, hilly town. A Sign read, "Welcome to Gowalia."

This little town had beautiful houses with manicured lawns.

"Hey, we have a lawn mower. I can use it to make some money," Douglas could not resist declaring.

The truck moved further and stopped at a traffic light. There was a big sign on a building that declared, "City Swimming Pool."

"Wow, look, Mom! I can swim here if we don't have a swimming pool in our new house," Sheena said, looking at it.

"You can't make money by swimming. Waste of time," Douglas advised his sister.

The truck moved further and stopped in front of a modest home. The driver came out and stood still.

Douglas and Sheena jumped out with joy.

"Hey, we made it!" The kids shouted together.

They begin unloading stuff.

"Driver, we need help. Please," Rubina requested.

"I can't help you. I told you, company's policy."

"But, sir, we would appreciate it as a special favor. I don't have a man in the house."

"I will do it," Douglas interrupted.

The driver reluctantly took out a handful of items. He helped with the big items later and threw some on the ground. The truck emptied, Rubina showed him the gas bill.

"And here is your remaining money. Thank you, Okay?" She said.

The driver took the money and drove away.

Some items were still sitting on the sidewalk as they slowly moved their belongings inside the house. Douglas and Sheena appeared sweaty, dirty, and exhausted.

CHAPTER 4
NEW KIDS IN TOWN

Five Years Later

The alarm clock went off exactly at six in Douglas's bedroom.

"Douglas, are you awake?" Rubina called from the kitchen.

"Yes, Mom," Douglas said.

Young Douglas got up wearing his pajamas. He straightened out his bed covers, walked toward the bathroom, and picked up a brush. He looked for some toothpaste but found a rolled-up, almost empty tube. He got a pencil, rolled hard from the bottom end to squeeze out enough paste onto his brush, and started brushing.

Douglas walked out and opened his garage. He sorted out his bundles of newspapers, put them in his bag, and hung it on his bike. Then he sprinted on his bike from house to house. He aimed and threw each copy to reach exactly in front of the door.

It was the weekend. Douglas mowed their neighbor's lawn. He was half done, and the elderly owner, Ruth, came out with some steaming-hot tea in a Styrofoam cup.

"Douglas, break time. Here is your hot tea."

Douglas sat down on the porch, wiping his sweat away and enjoyed his break.

"Thank you, Aunt Ruthy. You don't have to do this all the time."

"No problem. No problem at all," Ruth replied.

"How do you know I like tea?"

"Oh, I know it very well. You love tea."

Ruth took away the empty cup and left. Douglas finished the job. When Ruth returned, she looked at the lawn with satisfaction and then smiled.

"Good job," She complimented.

She gave him his payment envelope.

"Now it is finished quicker than when you were younger. See you next weekend," Ruth said.

Douglas said goodbye and dragged his lawnmower back to his garage.

After returning home, Douglas opened his garage. Everything inside was well organized. He dumped his money in a tin box marked "Minibank" sitting on the shelf.

He got dressed in his exercise gear. Following a workout video, he did some exercise.

He wiped the sweat from his face with a small towel. Then he went to the corner, picked up a pair of dumbbells, and did his thing.

A couple of teenage boys arrived in front. They peeked inside and watched him with curiosity. They were Smithy, a slim, lanky, mild-natured guy, and the big-mouthed, fat Bob.

"Hey, skinny boy, what are you doing?" Bob inquired.

"A little exercise," Douglas said.

Smithy looked at Douglas and said, "Hey, you can't call him names. It is his fitness that counts. He is slim not skinny, you fool."

"I don't mind. Say whatever, but say it with love," Douglas said.

"We have seen you doing this regularly. Can we join you?" Smithy politely suggested.

"Sure. Come on in," Douglas invited them.

They went inside.

"Wow, nice machines. We don't have equipment like this." Smithy was impressed.

"Now I know why you are so slim. You have muscles and a six pack too. Right, Slim Douglas?" Bob touched Douglas's tummy.

"You can always use my equipment," Douglas replied.

Both boys said, "Okay, we will pay you something."

"Why do you have to pay?" Douglas questioned.

"Machines wear out, man," Smithy explained.

The boys walked deeper into the garage with curiosity. Fat boy Bob tried the weights. He dropped one dumbbell on his toe.

"Aww ..."

"Watch out, please," Douglas warned.

$ $ $

One morning, while Douglas was working out on his treadmill, Smithy and Bob arrived.

Douglas stopped and said, "Guys, bad news. You can't work out here."

"Why?" The boys said together.

"Somebody gave me this." Douglas took out a wrinkled paper from his pocket.

"If I take your money, it becomes a business. City code says you can't have business in a residential zone." Douglas showed the paper to chubby Bobby.

"Bummer. But why? Come on; we will be quiet. Who is going to know?"

"Best to do what is right. You can't carry a burden of guilt all the time. Business can't grow and flourish that way," Douglas said.

"So what do you think?" Smithy interrupted Douglas.

"If you run a business, then you have to have a bookkeeper, accountant, lawyer, etcetera, etcetera, and pay the taxes."

"Man, you know a lot about business," Bob said.

Now Smithy, Bob's savvy acquaintance, came closer and whispered, "You know, Uncle George retired. His old auto shop is for rent, only a few blocks from here. We can rent that."

"Really?" Douglas was surprised.

"He also has some leftover exercise equipment."

"Good idea. Body shop, inside an auto body shop. Well, we will ask him. Also, more people can use it," Douglas declared.

"What would you call it?" Bob questioned Smithy.

"We will call it a Slim Douglas's Gym. Catchy, isn't it?"

And they dispersed.

Douglas walked into his kitchen.

"Those guys really want to work out in my gym. They think we can hide and lie about our business," Douglas said to Rubina.

"A lie does not go far. The truth prevails," Mom replied.

"But, Ma, how is someone going to know?"

"The truth always comes out in the end. It shouts from the roof, 'Hey, I am here!'"

"Yeah, yeah, I know." Douglas gave up.

"If you want to succeed, focus on the prize. It takes time, but victory will be yours."

"In that case, Mom, can we rent Uncle George's empty place for a gym?"

"You always put me on the spot. Do it at your own risk."

$ $ $

The next day, the sun was rising, and Douglas was sorting out the newspaper sections in the garage for delivery. He was preparing to ride his bicycle out, but he heard a rumbling sound, and everything started shaking. The bicycle slipped from his hands and fell.

Douglas shouted, "Mom, Sheena, come out! It is an earthquake! Run!"

Neighborhood people came out of their homes, shouting, "Earthquake! Earthquake! Get out of your homes!"

Some of them were wearing slippers, pajamas, and beanie hats. Some were covering themselves in blankets. People stood outside their respective homes on the sidewalks.

Parts of weaker houses were crumbling. Aftershocks continued. A police car arrived, making an announcement on the loudspeaker, "Get out of your homes. Emergency."

Douglas ran inside his house and brought out a couple of water bottles and a kettle. He hung it on his bicycle handles along with the newspapers on the carrier. He gave out hot tea in Styrofoam cups to the people who were just waking up.

A group of people were listening to portable radios, keeping them close to their ears.

"It is a seven-point-five grade earthquake. The epicenter is near the Santa Clara Valley. There is no news of damage yet."

A Humvee full of soldiers arrived with a bullhorn. A guy was sitting on top of the vehicle, asking, "Is everything all right?"

A fire broke out in one of the houses.

A soldier summoned a fire truck on his radio. The Humvee proceeded further.

All of a sudden, Douglas noticed a woman running out of her burning house. She came out into the street sidewalk shouting, "My dog! My dog!"

Douglas ran inside his house to get something.

"What are you doing?"

People were trying to stop him.

He ran inside without listening. He pulled out a crowbar from his open garage.

He ran to the woman's house and dug out the side of the window. He got inside and brought out a beautiful white puppy, clutched to his bosom. Everyone watching clapped. He had dark ash stuck on one of his cheeks. The other side had turned dark red with heat.

"Looks like aftershocks are easing down," someone said.

Pipes had busted. People were fetching water in buckets from a nearby stream. Children were applying their skills using hand trucks. Some dragged their containers with strings.

The next morning, Douglas was preparing to go on his newspaper route. A big bundle was lying near his feet. The visible headline on the front page read, "Brave Town Kid Saves A Dog."

Douglas mounted a load of newspapers on the bike and took off for the delivery.

$ $ $

On one beautiful weekend morning, Douglas and Sheena, both teenagers now, entered a beautiful town library. They went to the reference desk with a nameplate reading "Edith Kruzakowski."

The librarian, Edith, asked Sheena, "May I help you?"

"Oh yeah, where can I find cookbooks? Old classical organic recipe books please."

"May I ask you what you are going to do with them? I mean, what is your project?"

"We are doing research, ma'am. We want to create genuine recipes with ingredients like Grandma's."

The librarian searched in her computer and printed out a small list. She showed the list to Sheena and Douglas while making tick marks and circles around the important authors. Edith pointed them to the rear shelves.

"If you don't find anything there, then go to the basement for vintage books."

They went down and checked out the shelves with a great interest. They did not find exactly what they wanted, so they moved to the basement.

First, they looked at a vintage Chinese cookbook. Sheena went through the pages.

"Wow. Look, Dougy, somewhat like Grandma's ingredients. How do you pronounce it?"

They picked out a couple of old books. The pages had turned brown, and some were falling apart. Some had been repaired with plastic tape. They walked out with their books in tow.

Testing Day

In Douglas's home, plenty of sunlight was falling inside from the kitchen windows. A mild Pacific breeze was blowing the curtains. The kitchen counter was full of open recipe books.

There were scales and other measuring equipment in the corner. Bottles and cans from pint to gallon size filled with ingredients sat on the other end.

Sheena prepared the mixture by adding the ingredients to water while stirring. Douglas was still browsing various recipe books. He occasionally stopped, amazed.

"Wow. If Aryans were drinking this potion in ancient times, there must be something in it."

Sheena peeked inside the book. She looked at Douglas and said, "Aryans drank Somerus in the morning, while Mayans drank Chicha, a soupy, corn-based drink."

Douglas interrupted, "And what do Americans drink?"

"Coffee ..." both said together.

Douglas questioned Sheena, "Have you ever wondered why do Americans drink coffee?"

"Because there was no Boston Coffee Party." Sheena declares.

Sheena had made a good amount of brew in her kitchen. Douglas was watching her. She distributed equal-sized portions of liquid in marked clear plastic bowls. She added different types of spiced ingredients.

After mixing a while, she stopped, looked at her brother, and said, "And spike it with a pinch of spice like Grandma."

Douglas stepped away.

Sheena collected everything in a tray and made it ready. She came back and cleaned up the kitchen.

Douglas returned and asked, "What's next, Sis?"

"Experiment successful," replied Sheena.

"But you can't make good money if you do this kind of tiny business. You have to think bigger and smarter. Like Rockefeller and Carnegie," Douglas said.

"Come on! They are not in the food business. I only do it for my hobby. Maybe it will help me enter a culinary school."

"What I am trying to tell you is invention and investment. Never mind."

Sheena's kitchen looked like a testing lab. The countertop was shining clean. Bar chairs were all lined up. Sample drinks were ready to go.

The doorbell rang. Sheena got the door.

"Hi …"

She heard a loud, happy, girlish greeting in unison. Emily, Sheena's best friend, brought in three teenage girls from the neighborhood.

"Hi, Emily. Welcome all. Make yourself comfortable guys, please."

Sheena was holding a clipboard in her left hand. She walked over and picked up a sample.

"Let's try the first one, sample A. Emily, would you please help me pass on these samples?"

She gave them sample A to taste and passed outcome crackers. They marked their papers with a pencil.

Sheena continued, "Next one is B."

All tasted simultaneously.

"Ewe. Like too much ginger," the first girl said.

One of them ran to the sink and spit it out. They continued tasting and marking. They went from A to F. Sheena was tallying results.

"Wow. Two people have picked the same one," Sheena mentioned.

The girls looked at each other and burst into laughter.

"Awesome, what is it?" The second girl said.

"Same selection. Same one," the first girl added.

"Yeah … Good selection," they all said together.

They all picked up their stuff and proceeded to leave.

"Thank you guys for coming in. See you next time," Sheena acknowledged.

After they left, Douglas came in. Sheena sat down next to him with her clipboard to evaluate.

Sheena said, "It's a tie. I'm confused. Two of these drinks got equal points. The project still needs more work."

"Positive or negative, all data are important. They tell us the truth. Give us the right direction," Douglas opined.

$ $ $

One quiet night at the Din house, Douglas was eating ice cream in the kitchen. A half-gallon tub was open on the table. He looked at the ceiling, thinking deeply. Sheena walked in wearing her fancy pajamas. She had an empty glass in her hand. Her hair was out of place.

Sheena was surprised to see Douglas.

"Oh my God, Douglas, you are awake and eating ice cream late at night? I am going to tell Mom. Mom—"

"Stop it! I will catch you and beat you up."

She tried to run away. Douglas ran, grabbed her, and gave her a fake punishment.

"Tattletale. Grow up. Will you? I can't sleep. I'm thinking about what I should do to be successful."

"I know. First get a good education, and then apply for a good job. Simple," Sheena replied.

"Don't forget Dad said, 'My kids will make billions and billions.' Question is how?" Douglas lectured his sister.

"But Mom insists on education first."

"Then what?"

Douglas got up and went to the sink to wash his plate.

"Don't forget tomorrow is your contest. Better go to sleep."

Sheena filled her glass with water and left.

CHAPTER 5
GROWING UP

Douglas and Sheena arrived at Johnson Middle School. A couple of canvas bags were hanging on Douglas's scooter. He dropped off Sheena and her paraphernalia.

"Bye, Brother," Sheena bid Douglas goodbye.

"Good luck. Don't be shy. Give your best, "he replied.

"Okay."

"Determination is the GPS of success," Douglas gave Sheena some final advice and left.

A sign in front of the school read, "Junior Cooking Contest." A festival-like atmosphere prevailed inside a big hall.

Tables were lined up with pizza, hot dogs, hamburgers, Chinese and Mexican food, and all kinds of foods.

Sheena's table was in the middle. Her stall stood out compared to neighboring crummy and unorganized tables. She walked to the cafeteria and got a few big, empty containers on a cart.

Rival contestants looked down upon Sheena's drinks jokingly.

"Hey, bartender," a guy taunted Sheena, covering his mouth.

She had orange, apple, and pomegranate juices and many more exotic mixed drinks, along with milk and mineral water. She had placed a big ice bucket next to her table.

An attractive punch bowl with a colorful drink sat in the middle. It had a label hanging on the side. Labeled plastics cups filled with drinks were lined up.

A crowd of people went in and out of the hall to get free goodies. Their facial expressions predicted their likes and dislikes.

The first visitor came by Sheena's spot. She looked around, picked up a cup, and filled it from a huge plastic container equipped with a little faucet spout. She moved aside and enjoyed her drink.

A second, more talkative visitor came in.

"And what's the name of this outfit? Lemon Juice Hut or Juice Land? Juice, juice, and juice everywhere," the second visitor inquired.

He came closer and picked up a full cup. Then he read the various labels aloud, "Exotic Juice Delight, Morning Delight, Sunshine Deluxe, Tropical Nectar, Decent Drink, Muga Mix. Wow." The visitor was impressed.

He moved aside and then came back to Sheena with his cup. He took a sip.

"Cool," he said.

"Should be. There is ice in it," Sheena claimed.

The third visitor, a gentleman, came aside, sipping a drink.

"Ooh … tasty. What is it? Can I have more please?"

Sheena obliged.

"It is my exotic mixed fruit drink cocktail, sir."

"Oh yeah! What's the secret ingredient? Never tasted one like this before," he asked.

"It is only freshly squeezed fruit juices, spiked with a little coconut milk. That's all," Sheena explained.

The second visitor was listening while drinking. He stepped in and said, "And what booze did you put inside?"

"What?" Sheena was genuinely surprised. "Oh Nooooo. Nothing like that at all. Coconut milk only."

"Now your secret ingredient is not secret anymore," the second visitor joked.

In the meantime, a woman emerged from somewhere with two young children. The little rowdy one wanted a drink, Lime Lem, the lemonade-type drink. The child reached the container and opened the spout.

The mom screamed, "Stop it!"

She ran and closed the spout. The kid ran and tried to fill the cup. Improperly placed, the cup fell to the floor. The drink spilled all over from the open spout.

"What have you done?" The mom yelled.

Sheena rushed to retrieve the container. The mom and kids disappeared quietly.

No sooner did Sheena fix her mess than Chef Robert and his evaluation team appeared at the door. They started evaluating the food items on each table. Starting from the corner, they were coming closer to Sheena's stall.

"Oh my God, they are here!" Sheena cried out.

Quickly, the janitor came out and began to mop the floor. Sheena started crying. She sat down wondering what would happen now.

"God, I lost it. Everything went down the drain."

When the evaluation team arrived, the floor was still being cleaned. Looking at the distressed Sheena, they skipped the table and walked ahead.

The moderator, Robert, said, "We will come back later."

Sadly, Sheena helped the janitor. Contestants whose evaluation was finished were relaxing and chatting near their unorganized sloppy stalls. They looked down upon Sheena's condition. Some kids started collecting their empty containers.

"Forget it. You can't win," a neighboring kid said to Sheena sarcastically.

Sheena heard that inner voice in her mind. "Determination is the GPS of success."

Sheena quickly refilled the cups with the leftover drink saved under the table. She wiped the displayed jug clean to look more presentable.

The testing team came back. Sheena moved aside. All three inspectors picked up empty cups and filled their own samples. They evaluated them individually.

They marked their points on their clipboard. A couple of them moved aside and chatted. Their eyebrow gestures indicated agreement.

All three evaluators assembled briefly in the corner, covering their mouths with their hands.

The public address system announcement was on, "Folks, please, proceed to the assembly hall. The results will be announced within fifteen minutes."

Children and parents were anxiously waiting inside a school assembly hall. The principal and teachers came out on the stage.

The school principal said, "Ladies and gentlemen, students, welcome to our forty-second annual Junior Culinary Contest. Today, we have invited the popular restaurant chain owner, Chef Robert Mariano. Without further ado, I ask Robert to take over."

Robert greeted everyone with some kind of accent, "Hello, folks. All participants are winners. There are no losers. If not this time, you will be a winner the next time. Keep it up."

Robert dug out a piece of paper from his long coat pocket, saying, "Like last year, we have three prizes. All the recipes are wonderful."

He walked one step further and looked at the audience.

"Each winner, please come up and receive your prize. Here are the results. The third prize goes to vegetarian pizza by Tom King. Very tasty."

Tom got up and collected his prize. People applauded.

"Second prize goes to Rachel Smith for her innovative vegeburger. Slim down, everyone," Chef Robert continued.

Sheena joined in with the crowd for applause. Rachel jumped up, ran, and grabbed her prize box. Sheena held her head down and pondered.

Chef Robert spoke up in the tension-filled hall. "And last but not the least is … Drum roll, please. First prize winner is Sheena Din from the eighth-grade class for her tasty and nutritious exotic fruit drinks!"

The entire hall roared with applause. Sheena came forward, not believing that she had actually won. She took a bow and thanked everyone while receiving her prize of a thick recipe book.

"Thank you, sir, Mr. Moderator. I don't believe this. Thank you all. I am very, very grateful to my grandma for teaching me this."

Five Years Later

Gray smoke was visible from the rooftop of Rubina's factory. The whistle blew. At the main gate, workers were waiting in line to punch out and leave.

The chubby little graying lady Rubina was coming out of the door with the help of her cane. She was holding her plastic lunch box in the other hand. The purse was hanging on her arm.

She appeared tired as she walked out onto the sidewalk and disappeared inside a nearby supermarket.

$ $ $

At home, a grown-up Douglas was sitting at a table covered with envelopes and papers. He had some facial hair and a thin mustache.

Mother Rubina entered with a grocery bag. Douglas stood up enthusiastically. His mom came closer. Douglas picked up her bag and said, "Mom, guess what!"

Rubina quickly interjected, "Aren't you going to ask me how I am doing first and kiss me? Noooo, now that you are a big man."

Douglas pointed at himself with his thumb. "Mom, exciting news, your baby has been accepted at Wilson Business School near Boston."

Douglas showed her an envelope. Rubina did not pay much attention.

Douglas continued to boast, "The great educational institute, they are offering me a scholarship too. How about that?"

Rubina replied, "No, no, no. What?"

"I got lucky. You don't have to pay fees. Isn't that wonderful?"

"What is so wonderful about it? There are lots of schools around here."

"Saving money on the best college is not rocket science."

"Then what?" Rubina asked.

"It's pocket science, Mom."

"Boston? No, no. I don't want to miss my baby."

Douglas snapped, "Mom, let me go. I am late already. The application deadline is almost over. And it is the Wilson Business School. No other."

His mom had to agree.

A Boston Suburb

It was a daytime on the beautiful college campus of Wilson Business School. The campus was made of elegant buildings. There was a big hall in the center and a library in the corner. Dormitories, a gymnasium, and an open-air basketball court were located in the rear.

Douglas walked down the corridor and noticed an ad on the bulletin board: "Janitorial position available." He wrote down the information. He called from the wall phone while looking at his watch and proceeded to his dorm room.

After a while, Douglas came out of shower, half nude in a wet towel, showing his lanky but muscular body. He had wet hair, and his six-pack was visible.

He picked out clothes from the closet and dressed up in jeans and a T-shirt. Then he walked to the closet mirror in his slippers and took a good look at himself. He smiled and then spoke to the image.

"Gentlemen, I am your expert janitor. I am number one. Pick me. Pick me."

Douglas took out his shiny black pair of leather shoes from the closet, sat in a chair, looked at his shoes, and shouted, "Nooooo." He walked back and put them away. Next, he took out a pair of sneakers and put them on. He then left the room. He walked confidently toward the administrative office.

Two young candidates, Victor and Luis, were already waiting on a hallway bench outside the administrative office for a job interview.

The interviewer opened the door and peeked out. "Mr. Victor?"

The guy went in. A discussion went on. Moments later, the door opened.

"Thank you for coming. We will be in touch," the interviewer said.

Victor came out into the hallway and left.

A few moments later, the interviewer opened the door and announced, "Mr. Luis?" He invited Luis inside his office.

Luis was wearing overalls. He walked in. The door closed. The faint sound of conversation leaked out.

"The money is not enough," Luis mumbled.

The door opened, and both came out.

The interviewer said, "Thank you for coming in. We will let you know."

Douglas stood up well before his name was announced. The interviewer came out, smiling, and waved him in.

Upon entering, Douglas noticed a paper ball on the floor. Immediately, he picked it up and threw it into a dust bin, basketball style.

The interviewer watched this. He wrote something down. Next, Douglas playfully tried to lift a bag marked "Lift," with his muscular hands.

"No need. Not necessary. When can you start?" the interviewer asked.

He did not wait for the answer. He marks something down on his application and then shook his hand, saying, "Welcome aboard. Why did you apply late?"

"I had to convince my mom at home. She did not want me to leave after my dad passed away," Douglas said.

"Sorry to hear that. Then what happened?"

"I arrived late but lost my scholarship."

Right away, the interviewer marked down something more and thanked him for coming in.

CHAPTER 6
EDUCATION

Douglas's school had opened. He was sitting in the front row of a large lecture theater situated within a posh business school building. The lecturer began the class. He introduced himself first.

"My name is Baron Seth. Welcome to your new school. So, you have selected the best school, the school of business. People do farming, manufacturing, and construction or have a job to make a living. Some do business, but business is the best. Why? To make a lot of money, more than others, and pick on them? No. Business is a unique profession. It is a serious game. It requires all kinds of smarts. It's a challenge. It is an adventure. Some people think that 99 percent of new businesses fail in the first six months. Weak people and dreamers belong in that category. We want to be in the top 1 percent. That's why we are here."

Douglas raised his hand.

"Sir, so you make some money. But how do you keep it safe and growing?" He asked.

"Good question. That's what we are going to learn throughout the year," the lecturer replied.

The bell rang. Class was over. Douglas walked to his room.

In the evening Douglas dressed in overalls, was pushing a utility cart containing a broom, a mop, and a bucketful of other stuff within the dormitory hallway.

He went to the restroom and cleaned the toilet. He then cleaned the floor with the brush and mopped and wiped clean the mirror. He replenished the toilet paper rolls and paper towels, which he pulled out from a tiny closet.

He walks to the center area, pushing his electric vacuum cleaner, and vacuumed the carpet. Everything looked immaculate.

Four Years Later

Bearded Douglas was doing his final janitorial shift.

"Last cleaning, eh? Can't imagine. Where did the time go?" a passerby commented.

"Oh yeah, the last cleaning. Gives me a little change. Got me through four years. A nice workout too," Douglas agreed.

"Ready for the commencement? See you tomorrow, man."

Douglas put his equipment away in the closet. Then he walked down the corridor. He looked outside through a huge glass window. College kids were relaxing. Some were sitting leisurely near the fountain, chatting, horsing around, drinking, and smoking. Girls were playing badminton; some were throwing a Frisbee on the lawn.

"Friday Is Graduation Day" signs were hanging everywhere.

"Come one; come all. Governor Mulligan presiding. Gowns are available in the gym and from the college bookstore and local town stores."

Douglas went down to his room and prepared for his valedictorian speech. He started reading from a library book *Great Valedictorians* as he lay down. He went to the library.

Douglas was sitting with an oversized file in the college library. The title read "Public Speaking." He carefully turned the old, broken pages and read with concentration. Occasionally, he took down notes. He got up in a hurry because he had to pick up his sister.

Douglas was waiting inside Logan Airport. Sheena came out through the arrival gate. Douglas ran and hugged her.

"Welcome to Boston, Sis."

Following her was Sheena's best friend, a pretty young lady.

"Douglas, meet my friend, Emily," Sheena said. "Emily, my brother, Douglas."

They shook hands, feeling shy.

"I know you. You and Sheena are going to the same class, right? Thanks for coming," Douglas said.

The three were driving away. Douglas talked to Sheena.

"Since you want to be a culinary expert, we are going to visit some exotic restaurants tonight. My treat."

They arrived at the lakeside James River Hotel.

"This is where you are going to stay."

Later that evening, they visited downtown Boston. They sat at a city sidewalk café. After that, they went to another place called Mediterranean Galore across the street. The waiter came and gave them the menu. They enjoyed a fancy dish. Sheena talked to the waiter.

"May I ask you a question? What is the special ingredient in this item?"

The waiter was confused. He thought for a moment. "Gee, I don't know. Only the chef knows." He walked backward slowly and left.

"Never mind," Sheena said.

The waiter came back with the chef.

"Good evening, folks. My name is Chef Pizzini. May I help you?"

"Not necessary. I liked your dish. Since I am a culinary student, I was wondering what was inside," Sheena said.

The chef approached her. He shook her hand and insisted she follow him.

Both went to the kitchen. Douglas and Emily were left alone. Everything became dead quiet. Emily was blushing.

The interior of the chef's kitchen was fairly neat. Kitchen gadgets and utensils were hanging in order. Most of them were new, while the old ones had dents and carbon stuck in their dents.

The chef was explaining her tricks of the trade. Sweet nothings. Occasionally, Sheena nodded her head in agreement.

The waiter came back to Emily and Douglas.

"Would you join us, please?" the Chef invited.

They got up and followed the waiter. Both started talking while walking.

"So, Emily, may I ask what are you up to study-wise? I understand you must have finished or are about to finish your studies."

"No, I still have one more semester to go. Now I am also into modeling and advertising."

They went inside and watched until the chef's demonstration was over.

After Sheena thanked the chef and shook hands, they left.

Graduation Day

Sheena and Emily got out of the taxi in front of Boston Community Hall, climbed the steps, showed their passes to the attendant, and picked up brochures from a youngster. He showed them the entrance. They went inside and took their seats.

It was a large gathering. Signs greeting students were present everywhere.

"Congratulations, New Graduates!"

There were a huge number of excited students sitting in the front. They were wearing their graduation gowns and pointy square hats. All were anxious to graduate. Sheena stood up and tried to locate Douglas in the front-row area. She did not find her brother and gave up.

"I don't know where he would be. They all look alike," Sheena said to Emily.

The organizer came on the stage. Students shouted, "Heyyyy …" The flurry of activity was increasing within the hall.

The governor of Massachusetts presided. The college band finished its gig. The director stood up and began, "Honorable Governor, ladies and gentlemen, and of course new graduates to be, welcome to our ceremony. Congratulations, new graduates. Now I would request the honorable governor say a few words."

Smiling, the governor stood up, walked out in front, gave a few words of advice, and ended with, "I hereby declare all of you graduates. Good luck. Go out and be successful."

As soon as the initial ceremony was over, students got up, shouted, and threw their hats in the air, making a loud noise, "Heyyyy ..."

The director got up and requested the valedictorian, Douglas Din, to take over.

Clean-shaven and well-groomed, Douglas walked onto the stage confidently. Everybody clapped. The handsome and confident young man began, "Honorable Governor, Dean Dr. Langford, faculty members, families, friends, invited guests, and, of course, dear fellow new graduates, what a wonderful day it is today. Today we are climbing an important peak, one of many summits we have to conquer in our lives. We have not arrived here alone but only by standing on the shoulders of the others."

Douglas walked toward the front of the stage with the mic."Folks, we thank our wonderful dean Dr. Langford and his magnificent staff. Only by their guidance and leadership have we come to see this day. We are, of course, grateful to our friendly administration office staff, our maintenance staff, and our cafeteria and kitchen staff. Thank you all."

Douglas stepped back and went to the podium.

"So, my dear Wilsonians, today we have become business graduates, and we are proud because we feel so unique. Most important is that we pledge to apply diligently whatever nitty-gritty tricks of the trade we have learned. Now we will have a chance to share our goodness with humanity. That is called living life, real life, and living life truthfully, fruitfully, and at the end proudly saying, 'Mission accomplished. 'Bravo, good luck, and God speed." He received a huge round of applause.

Then he stepped down from the podium. The ceremony was soon over, and people mingled to find their loved ones. Douglas came swimming through the crowd to find Sheena and Emily.

Sheena walked up, hugged him, and said, "Congratulations."
Emily shook his hands, bowed a little, and said, "Congratulations."
All three walked out together.

Back Home in California

Douglas was sitting on his couch, checking out the *Wall Street Journal*. Rubina looked at Douglas's graduation picture on the wall and said, "So, now you have a degree. Find a job, and start working, young man."

"I have a number of job offers coming in the mail," Douglas replied proudly.

"What type?"

"One is from a Wall Street area bank; the other one is from an international financial Corporation."

"Really? So."

"But I have a steaming-hot, unique desire."

"What do you mean?"

"I want to start my own business."

"What type of business?"

"Selling tea."

"Have you lost your mind? Why?"

"Why not?"

"After all this education, you are going to sell tea?"

"Ma, not just tea. The best tea. Exotic tea. Healthy tea. Super tea. Blended tea, money-making tea."

"A tea vendor? Huh …"

"There is a lot of difference between a tea stall and a tea business. Understand?"

"I feel insecure."

"Insecurity breeds failure."

"Answer is no."

She left the room but came back feeling guilty.

Douglas said, "I have worked so hard and come up to here. Will you at least let me do one thing of my own?"

"I know you are your own man. You won't take my advice. I should not interfere with your plans." Rubina gave him a hug.

"Thanks, Mom. Remember, Dad wanted us to fulfill his dream. Let me give it a shot and get it done."

"But remember your dad lost everything."

"There is no fun like owning your own business," Douglas declared proudly.

$ $ $

On a remote highway shoulder, Sheena's car was stalled. Its hood was open. Steam was wafting outside slowly. She pathetically tried to flag down the passing cars.

"Sir, do you have water?" She requested.

A few of them slowed down with curiosity. Some didn't even look at her. A few cursed at her. Some laughed at her when she inquired.

Finally, one old African American truck driver stopped. He picked up a gallon of jug of antifreeze from the floor. Quickly, he passed the antifreeze jug to Sheena through the window.

"How much, sir?"

There was no answer. The truck driver took off quickly and got out, clearing the stalled traffic behind him.

$ $ $

Douglas was eagerly waiting outside their home when Sheena arrived. She came out with a Navin Fashions clothing box under her arm and two gallon jugs of antifreeze.

"What happened? What took you so long?" Douglas inquired.

"You won't believe it. I went shopping, and the engine ran out of antifreeze. The car stalled. I had it serviced just last week."

"Why two gallons?"

Sheena explained, "The truck driver who gave me his antifreeze for free had to drive away because of the stalled traffic."

She proudly looked at the jug of antifreeze.

"When I give away this gallon to someone needy, then we will be even."

$ $ $

At night, Douglas and his graying mom were relaxing in their living room. Rubina's walking cane was lying next to her.

Sheena entered dressed in her graduation outfit and said, "How do I look, guys? Do you like it?"

"Wonderful. When is your graduation?" Rubina questioned.

"Next Friday afternoon. Don't you remember? Dougy, are you going with me?" Sheena inquired.

"Where? To your commencement? Of course."

Douglas turned to his mom. "Mom, would you join us? Make your baby girl happy. How is your leg now?"

"So-so. I would try to come though."

Delighted, Sheena gave her mom a hug and left the room hopping.

CHAPTER 7

BUSINESS MIND

Sheena and Rubina were relaxing in their living room where Sheena's fresh graduation photo was clearly visible on the wall. Douglas entered through the door.

"Guys, if you have a few minutes, I would like to show you something interesting today. We will be right back."

"Oookay." Suspicious, Rubina and Sheena agreed.

The three were driving away. Sheena had started feeling awkward.

"What is it? Where are you taking us? Give us a hint."

"You will see it in a minute."

They were cruising in the car.

"It is not too far," Douglas assured them.

"Aha, I smell something. When did you make the deal?" Rubina asked.

"A couple of weeks ago."

"Ye … ah, that's why you were going in and out of home so frequently. Now I understand."

Rubina looked at Sheena. "He is exactly like your dad. Never tells me anything."

"Ma, nothing was finalized, so I couldn't announce anything," Douglas explained.

"I always knew it. Dougy is going to do something adventurous," Sheena said.

"But you have to be careful," Rubina alerted him.

When they arrived in front of a coffee shop, the car stopped. They stayed inside.

A big sign announced, "Opening soon! Visit our coffee shop. Drink tea, and have a taste of a lifetime. Proprietor: Douglas Din."

"Wow!" Sheena pointed at the sign and said. "Mom, proprietor." She giggled and slapped her brother on the back with love.

Rubina critically looked at the shop and said, "What is this? Too small."

"Not a chance for billions. Big risk," Sheena added.

"Thanks for the encouragement. Do you want to go inside? Nothing is organized yet," Douglas answered.

"No, it is okay for now."

"Jobs are better security," Rubina expressed.

They drove back.

New Business

One morning after his business was established, Douglas walked to the SlimDoug enterprise tea stall from the street. He opened the store and walked inside. The open sign was turned around from the glass window. Employees followed him.

Customers started lining up. Douglas intermittently joined to serve customers along with his employees. Busy, Douglas slowed down at the end of the day.

The last four or five customers were left. Douglas breathed easy.

"How are you today, sir?" He talked to an elderly customer.

"Good, very good. Call me Roby Batt. I guess you are the owner."

"Yes indeed."

"We don't have this kind of tea in our neighborhood. I came here all the way from Sun Drive Boulevard," Roby Batt told Douglas.

"Really?"

"Many of us come from that area. Can you start a stall over there?"

"I also come from downtown. I think Main Street has more traffic. Start one over there," a bystander put in his five cents.

"Very good idea. We will think about that."

At the end of the day, Douglas's young helper, Jimmy looked at the clock. It was 10:00 p.m. He closed the door and turned the sign to "Closed."

Douglas went to the corner and counted the money. He came back.

"Jimmy, Elijah, Sandy, Mark, please come here," Douglas invited all near him.

All four young employees stopped sweeping and cleaning. They stepped up to the cashier's counter wondering and feeling insecure.

"Nice job, guys. It has been six months and customers like your work. Me too. Keep up the best show."

He opened the ledger book, looked inside, and announced, "From next week, all of you will have a raise of one dollar per hour."

Then Douglas stepped out from the counter area. He went to his office and came back with a bunch of small white envelopes in his hands.

"Who wants to buy a car? Take this, and save it for your new car, Sandy."

Sandy quickly opened the envelope and pulled out a fifty-dollar bill.

"Thank you, Mr. Douglas."

Douglas continued, "Now, Mark, your baby is sick. Buy her some good medicine." He went to Mark and gave him a small envelope.

Mark looked inside and found a crisp fifty-dollar bill. He smiled. "Gee, thanks. Never thought of this," Mark said.

"Jimmy, you have been serving here the longest. Would you be willing to become the manager of our new tea stall? Here is your incentive."

Douglas also gave him an envelope with a fifty-dollar bill stuck inside.

Surprised, Jim said, "Really? Sure! Why not? It will be an honor. Appreciate it."

"And who got mugged last week at night?" He also passed Elijah his envelope. "This is for you, Elijah."

Grand Opening

Douglas ventured to open another store downtown. The stall front was decorated with balloons and ribbons along with an attractive sign at Sun Drive: "Coming soon, Slim Douglas Tea Stall. Free tea to the first one hundred customers."

Excited, enthusiastic people had started forming a line. The crowd was building up. Customer Robby Batt, who suggested starting a new restaurant, had the honor of cutting the ribbon.

News media rushed in. They were trying to set up their equipment in the front of the store. A newsman, holding his mic, was eager to take an interview. Douglas appeared in the door wearing an apron and a hat.

"Are you the owner?" The reporter asked him.

"Yes, sir."

The reporter said, "We are from GWC TV. Why didn't you tell us earlier? We would have reported it in a full-length segment?"

"It is just a stall, nothing special."

"Just a stall? It is a super stall. Look at the people you have gathered. There must be something." He pointed at the crowd and continued, "You have created a tea mania. This is the talk of the town. Do you mind if I take an interview?"

"Okay. Better be a brief one."

Cameraman and the producer cleared up the space and created a mini set.

The reporter said, holding a mic, "Live from Sun Drive. Folks, a brand-new tea stall is opening here by public demand. I am with the young proprietor named Douglas Din." He pointed at the unusual business sign, which read, "Slim Douglas's Tea Stall."

Then he asked Douglas, "May I ask you about this unique sign here?"

"When I was younger, I used to be thin. My peers were teasing me by calling me 'Skinny Douglas.' Isn't it a catchy name for a business?" he explained.

"Very few businesses are opened by public demand. People have been lining up since dawn to pick up their free cup of tea."

The reporter walked toward the crowd. The cameraman followed.

"Folks, we are interviewing this young entrepreneur named Douglas ... a future tea king." He walked back to Douglas. "Let's meet the owner. Douglas, how old are you?"

"Twenty-five."

"Wow. What inspired you to start this stall?"

"The people. Well, many customers want to have a stall near them. Therefore, we are venturing to have one right here."

"Wonderful. Good luck in your business. Viewers, go try healthy spiced tea." The reporter sipped a cup of tasty tea. "Wow. Good body. No crummy bags to hang. And tastes wonderful. It should be illegal. Just kidding."

He walked toward the crowd and said, "Let me add one more thing, folks: Mr. Douglas is an exercise buff and is also involved in his gym business."

People around the neighborhood were also watching TV. They jumped out of their chairs and rushed to the venue. Customers lined up with money in their hands. When they reached the inside, they realize it was free tea that day.

The reporter said, "Do you know, it was free tea for the first one hundred, but now it is for the first two hundred. The proprietor was so impressed, he revised it."

People said, "It tastes so good, we will pay."

Douglas was busy inside his tea stall. Across the street, two other store owners were watching live TV. They saw newsmen questioning Douglas. The TV camera showed a couple of other food places also. Two guys were talking about Douglas.

"That guy has also started a second tea stall. New businesses fold in six months. He will close down soon," the first guy said.

In the next block, another jealous guy's stall and cafeteria appeared to be empty. Tables on the sidewalk were without patrons.

"Find out what his trickery is. We will challenge him in the court if he hurts our business," the angry-looking second guy said.

He walked up to the third businessman next door. "We are already in contract with our supplier Tropical Tea Trading." He looked up thinking. "I am wondering why this new guy's tea tastes so good. And why is it always crowded? Why does nobody interview us?"

"I don't know. Maybe he has stolen our recipe from somewhere?" The first guy said.

"Have you seen him over here anytime? I think he is the one who was roaming around here. Sometimes he took away cups full of tea with him. Perhaps he got it analyzed in the lab," the second guy wondered.

"Aha. There you go. You nailed it. Let's sue him. I am going to our Tropical Tea Traders Association meeting tonight. We will strongly pursue it."

In the city, Skinny Douglas Tea stalls were busy. Trucks marked "Slim Douglas Tea" were running all around the city.

There was a sign: "Have you tried fruit and vegefritters. They are made with onions, potatoes, sweet peppers, bananas, and cucumbers. Try them today. Also taste KofiTea, a novel idea along with our house beverages."

One late night, almost all the stores in the street are closed. A police car arrived, flashing its lights. It sounded a brief alarm. The officer talked to the man working on his truck tires. It was Douglas.

"Whose truck is this?" Police officer asked.

"It is my truck, Officer."

"What happened?"

"Flat tire. Third time this week. Sir, I work right here in my stall."

"Do you want to report it?"

"No, sir. It could be a rowdy kid or one of my customers or just a coincidence. Not sure. Never mind."

After the police left, Douglas proceeded home.

Douglas arrived at home. Tiptoeing, he entered the kitchen and found his prepared dish on the table. He went to a microwave oven. Rubina and Sheena both dashed in.

"What happened? Why are you so late?" Both questioned.

"Someone slashed my tire. Not one but two. I had to take a taxi."

"Don't you understand people envy you? They hate your success," Rubina explained.

"Okay, Mom, calm down, everything will be all right."

Rubina angrily lectured, "It is a jungle out there. I am telling you. We are not the business type. Stop everything. Find a job. I am so insecure."

$ $ $

On a fine morning, Douglas was going to his Slim Douglas Gym. He was driving down the highway wearing his workout suit. He came across several Douglas Gyms along the way.

Many people headlined up to go inside for a workout. He also saw on the highway a brand-new bill board saying, "Buy Slim Douglas health products. Slim Douglas Enterprises also makes Spring Flower, White Peacock, and Busy Bee brands of teas."

He arrived in front of a funky gymnasium and went inside.

It was a huge hall. A classroom was located in the corner area. Lockers in the opposite corner were visible. The hall was full of exercise equipment. People were working out on nicely set up exercise machines.

Douglas had just finished showing a video to the newcomers inside the classroom. He answered the participants' questions. A sign said, "First month free. No obligation."

Pictures of great athletes were hanging on one wall. On another wall, there were pictures of athletes who had lived more than a hundred years.

There was a line under the picture: "Live a copy book life. Live large. Live forever."

Also on the wall, somebody had made chalk graffiti under Douglas Din's picture: "He never smoked."

The next plaque said, "Fresh air, clean water, nutritious food, light exercise, clean thoughts, and good deeds beget a perfect life."

$ \$ \quad \$ \quad \$ $

It was a new day. Douglas was driving his mini truck to work on the California highway through morning traffic. He noticed a brand-new Lincoln Continental stalled on the shoulder with flashers turned on.

A well-dressed elderly couple was standing outside, desperately looking for some help. Their young driver son, dressed in a dark suit, was standing a little further away with his head down.

Douglas stopped, rolled down his window, and asked the elder.

"Need help, folks?"

"Is it possible for you to drop us off at the airport? We are afraid we will miss our flight."

"No problem. If you don't mind my truck, the airport is right on my way. Come on down," Douglas replied.

They loaded up their luggage and took their seats. Enthused, Douglas drove away.

"Where are you heading to, young man?" The elder inquired.

"I am going to work, sir. I have a small café downtown. I am going into my dad's business; he died about ten years ago."

"Sorry to hear that. We are flying to Tucson to see my sick ninety-five-year-old mom."

"May I ask, what happened to your new car?" Douglas inquired.

"Nothing. My son forgot to put gas in it. You know, kids."

As soon as they arrived at Gowalia Airport, Douglas turned his flashers on and parked his mini truck. He helped the lady step out and then took the luggage out from back of the truck.

"Thank you, son."

"Safe flight," Douglas responded.

Douglas started to leave.

"How much do we owe you?" The elder asked.

"Nothing." He insisted, feeling shy.

He smiled and drove away. The elder looked at his truck license plate and marked something down in his pocket diary.

A Month Later

Douglas received a special envelope in his mailbox. A business card dropped out of the envelope. He wondered and read the greeting card.

"Thank you for the ride to the airport the other day. Good luck with your business. If you have any business questions, feel free to contact me. Thank you again. From Maestro, Secretary Department of Commerce."

Douglas got busy with expanding his new business. A brand-new outfit named SDE Beverage Shop was opening in the town. A cup and a saucer were sitting on the roof, inviting customers. A fan blew a white ribbon, depicting wafting steam from inside.

The dynamic manager, Sandra, was standing in. People inserted their cards and punched their order numbers inside a drive-in kiosk. They filled the desired size cup with a smile.

Inside, there were pitchers of fresh cold water filled with floating shiny ice cubes, as well as milk, orange juice, apple juice, tropical fruit juice, sports drinks, spiced tea, and coffee.

The menu on the inside wall revealed ginger tea, cinnamon tea, vanilla tea, rose tea, a coffee-tea cocktail, basil tea, rosemary tea, butterfly tea, honeybee tea, Busy Bee tea, and a lot more. Cars drove to the window.

People enjoyed fancy pastries along with a drink. Some bought freshly cut fruit salad.

Outside, in the drive-in lane, there was a sophisticated menu board stand.

People ordered directly with their cell phones, asking the kiosk machine in the drive-in lane to fill their orders. They paid with credit cards, and the robotic tray slid out from the kiosk in the next window.

CHAPTER 8

DEEP VENTURES

Somewhere in Central America

A ferryboat, full of village people, was rapidly cruising toward a remote mountainous island. One of the passengers was Douglas. He was dressed in a business suit but wore no tie. Douglas wanted to expand his business internationally.

Eager-looking Douglas was carrying a briefcase. The boat was docked. He got off.

A shower of heavy rain passed through. The rain stopped. The water quickly drained out. The sun came out. The flowery mountain terrain looked pleasantly green.

Douglas started walking. On his way, he came across local native Indians dressed in colorful handmade outfits.

The natives raised their hands, saying, "Hau."

Douglas bowed in return.

While he was walking, on the way each native stopped and joined to give Douglas a traditional respectful Indian greeting. Douglas saw a totem pole, tepees, cornfields, and more Indian things on his way.

An elderly chief came riding a beautiful, long-haired white mustang. The chief had a pure native look. He was wearing beads and feathers.

The chief came closer, curious.

"Who are you? Why are you here, young man?" The chief inquired with his accent.

"I am from North America. I sell tea. And I have come here to ask about your beautiful land," Douglas politely replied.

"No, no, no. Mi no sell island."

"May I know the reason, Chief?"

"This land is my land. Go back to your country, gringo. This is my country. Go away."

"Chief, I am not interested in grabbing your land. I want to go higher up in life."

Respectfully, Douglas kept his head down and looked at the ground.

The chief ordered the cadets, "Get rid of him."

"Wait. Let me explain it to you, Chief. We are in the tea business. We want to experiment and grow the world's best tea, like nobody has ever seen. That's all," Douglas pleaded.

He walked back and forth while talking cautiously. The chief was closely watching him.

Douglas continued, "You know tea requires subtropical, hilly, mountainous soil. A location where moisture is present but extra rainwater quickly drains out. You are blessed. Capisce?"

"Me capisce everything. Todo. Gringo wants to cheat us and make money. No more. No way. Get out. Go away. Buh-bye."

The chief climbed back on and patted his horse, saying, "Hey, Volley, ho."

The chief rode his horse away. Waiting under a nearby tree, Douglas put his briefcase behind his back with two hands and walked up to the chief, showing his frustration to convince him.

"Listen, Chief, sorry if I was direct. I am really, really interested. Do you have anything else to sell?"

Douglas moved even closer. The chief continued listening.

"There will be a lot of jobs for your reserve ... I mean for your community's people. And they will be happy," Douglas continued.

Again, Douglas started pacing to and fro, thinking. He talked to the chief.

"Let me tell you, Chief, there is plenty of tea-growing land available all over the world."

"Then go there."

"The only reason I don't want to go to China, India, and Sri Lanka is that it would be difficult to commute from here."

Douglas looked at him with a begging gesture to convince him.

"It will be good karma. Only this much I have to respectfully request of you. Please."

The chief brought his horse closer to Douglas and pointed. "Would you be interested in another island just like this? Nobody lives there. Only a few miles from here," he told Douglas softly.

"How much are you selling it for?"

"No selling. Hundred-year lease and 50 percent partnership," the chief said.

Douglas said, "You will have to work if you become a partner, you see."

"No partner. Okay fifty-year lease."

Douglas leaned forward and shook his hand. He said, "Okay. Done. Let your lawman and my man do the paperwork."

Both departed feeling happy.

A Few Months Later

Within no time, there was a lush garden, looking beautiful on a bright, sunny day on the Central American island. Sections of nice square beds were looking wonderful. A series of experimental plants were growing in the front.

Hardworking laborers were busy. Women had their head covers on. They were wearing beautiful decorative beads. Girls were carrying elongated baskets on their backs.

A tractor like truck dropped off a dozen or so workers at their work stations. Huge farm machinery was in action all around.

On the other end, a crew was collecting ripe tea leaves in makeshift cloth bags the old-fashioned way. Trucks took them to the refining and packaging shed.

Packed boxes were stacked in the truck for delivery.

"Bueno. Folks, keep up the good work. It is not only a job; it is service. We have leased this garden," Douglas encouraged the workers before returning.

$ $ $

After returning home, the first thing Douglas did was go to the office of the Tea Traders Association. He walked up to a mature lady clerk at the reception counter. Her name plate read "Margie Walters."

"I am Douglas Din. I own the SDE franchise. I want to be a member," Douglas declared.

"How did you hear about us? There is no room for new applicants. We are full," the clerk said.

"So what should I do, ma'am?"

"I don't know. Apply later, maybe."

She looked away. Frustrated, Douglas slowly stepped back and said, "But, miss, I want to legitimately file my papers."

"Mr. Jackford, the president of the association, will not add more new members."

She removed her glasses, stared at him, and said, "Do you have any references? You put your mark everywhere. An inquiry is against you about your mysterious dealings. Never mind."

"What? I had called the president a few days ago, and he asked me to check in here."

"Drop your application in that box. I have more important things to do. Okay?" The clerk uttered carelessly.

Frustrated, Douglas prepared to leave. The clerk stopped him.

"Wait! Don't call and bother us. We will let you know," she commanded while putting her glasses on.

Douglas turned around and reluctantly moved away.

$ $ $

One night, Douglas's SDE stall's lights were turning off one by one to close down.

"Good night, Mr. Douglas," the employees said as they walked out of the door.

"Bye," Douglas responded.

As the last man out, Douglas closed his door, holding his bag of cash in his left hand. He walked to his mini truck.

A shadow appeared behind him. Suddenly, a tall guy with a dark hat attacked him to grab his money bag. He had a large knife in his right hand.

"Hey, you, give me your bag, you fool, or else!" the mugger got him from behind.

"Wait, brother. I am giving it to you. Leave me alone," Douglas said.

The guy tried to grab his bag.

"Give it to me, you punk, or else!" the mugger yelled.

Thinking fast, Douglas focused and grabbed him below his wrist tightly. He jerked him with his hip. The guy's knife went flying off. Douglas twisted his hand, and the guy's body turned around. He fell flat on the ground. His hat rolled, tumbling down. Douglas pressed him with his knee.

The mugger said, "Noooo!"

Douglas left him alone, ran, and got into his truck. The guy got up, picked up his knife, grabbed his hat, and ran away.

Douglas arrived home late at night with a bandage on his neck. Rubina and Sheena came out running.

"What happened? Why are you late? What is this cut?" Rubina and Sheena questioned him.

"Nothing special, a guy wanted my money."

"My God, a mugger. Did you give it to him?" Sheena asked.

"No, I gave him a karate chop and grabbed his wrist tightly, shoved him hard with my hips, twisted his wrist, and threw him on the ground. I pressed his arm with my knee," Douglas described.

"Then what?"

"I came home."

"Did you beat him up, Brother?"

"No, karate is for self-defense."

$ $ $

It was evening in Douglas's house. He was reading the *Wall Street Journal* in his living room.

He turned to the legal business section on the last page. He noticed a weird headline at the top: "Business Tea Trading Association Sues Local Man for Stealing Their Recipe." Douglas read this and jumped up, shouting, "Oh really? No, no, no, it is my own research. Are you kidding me? God, what a bunch of idiots. All right, I will see you all in court."

A few days went by. Douglas was busy working in his business kitchen. A police van arrived in front. The sheriff jumped out, carrying his notepad. He came into Douglas's tea stall.

"Who is this Douglas?" he inquired.

Douglas came running out from inside the kitchen area.

"My name is Douglas, Officer. May I help you?"

The sheriff answered in awe, "I have an arrest warrant against you."

"What? But why?" Douglas was surprised.

"You are a fraud. Plaintiffs complain that you are trying to run away."

"What? Really? Lies."

"All your businesses are frauds. Per US Code Title 18, you have a right to remain silent."

The sheriff took out a pair of handcuffs. He shouted at the employees, "Drop everything, and come out. Listen, all, the shop is closed and locked."

Douglas sized up the situation, made a quick phone call to his friend Smithy, and then put the phone back in his pocket.

$ $ $

At the other end, Sheena entered the house, holding her cell phone to her ear. Her voice cracking, Sheena said, "Mom, stay calm. Smithy called. I have bad news."

"What? Oh my God, what happened?" Rubina yelled.

When Sheena and Rubina arrived, a crowd of people was creating chaos in front of the shop. Sheena parked the car opposite Douglas's shop. Both came out. Rubina walked with her stick, carrying her bag and rushing toward the stall.

"Come on, Mom! Follow me. Hurry up."

Rubina dragged behind Sheena, limping.

"Is he all right? I kept telling him not to do this."

Outside his stall, the protesters were shouting profanity and insulting Douglas. Vandalism on the outside wall was visible. It was marked with words like *fraud*, *thief*, *criminal*, and *conman*. Rubina rushed in front. She glanced at the crowd.

"Leave him alone! What did he do? You are all going to pay for this. My boy did nothing wrong."

"Stay away, lady," the police shoved Rubina.

"You cannot falsely arrest him. This is not Burma. There is no crime. God."

Rubina slowly backed away from the police barricade, crying.

Associates closed everything and locked it. Police sealed the lock. Embarrassed and confused, the employees came out into the street, wandering around.

The sheriff's deputy ordered Douglas, "Hands behind your back."

The deputy clicked the handcuffs and put on leg irons. He took him inside the van and started doing his paperwork while keeping the van door open.

Sheena ran in, screaming, "What are you doing? Oh God, no! Please no!"

Rubina fell to the ground and passed out. Her cane flew off, so did her bag. Sheena ran back and pulled out her cell phone.

"Nine-one-one, we have an emergency ..." Sheena kept talking.

The ambulance arrived sounding the horn. They took Rubina inside. The Noxford County Police van door slammed closed. The van went one way, while Rubina's ambulance went the other way.

In the corner, a mysterious man paid lined up hooligans their remuneration. People dispersed. The place was deserted. Sheena was left alone.

Broken down, sweaty Sheena dragged herself toward the shop, carrying her mom's bag and cane. She sat down on the steps, clasping her hands together. She did not want to leave.

Smithy arrived on a motorbike. He took his helmet off and hopped off.

"What happened?" He inquired.

Sheena stood up and hugged him. She was sobbing.

"Don't cry. I heard it. Let's go home," Smithy said.

"No, let's go to the hospital first," Sheena suggested.

$ $ $

The sheriff's wagon arrived in front of the Noxford County Jail. The sheriff's deputy, the assistant, and Douglas walked in. They met the prison warden.

In the corridor, they passed through a series of cells with dark metal bars in the front. A bed and an open toilet were visible in each cell. A mental inmate was sleeping in a fetal position in a corner floor.

They found another inmate vomiting in a cell's toilet bowl. They went further. The officer slid open a squeaky metal door.

"This is your place," the prison officer told Douglas.

They removed his handcuffs. The attendant gave him an orange prison uniform."

A barber came in with his tool case and gave Douglas a quick haircut. The warden banged the gate closed. After a while, Douglas, with a crew cut, was wearing the prison uniform, writing something on a notepad. A few loose papers were lying around.

CHAPTER 9
LEGAL TROUBLES

Douglas was taken to a small room within the jail for questioning. Crew-cut Douglas was sitting right in the middle of a room, wearing his orange jail overalls. A large light bulb was hanging over his head.

"So tell me how you stole the recipe, punk?" The officer demanded.

A sweaty-faced Douglas replied, "Sir, I have not stolen or copied any recipe."

The officer got mad.

"Don't give me that crap, you conman."

He hit the baton on the table. The light gets brighter and hotter.

"Tell me, where did you get the idea? Don't waste my time, you idiot. You are not going to get away," the officer threatened, using more abusive words.

"Grandma. My grandma taught and inspired us to cook. Recently, I bought a piece of land to experiment with my new ideas …" Douglas explained.

A large hanging light bulb became the brightest and hottest. Douglas started sweating profusely.

The officer demanded, "Don't tell me a fairytale. Tell me the truth. You cannot escape the long arm of the law."

Bright sunlight prevailed outside the jailhouse building the next morning. A roof and a wall were being repaired. Inmates were working and forming a line. Douglas was standing on a ladder-like structure, catching cinder blocks one by one and passing them to the next guy on the top. He was sweating and had started experiencing a little shortness of breath.

The wall was just finished. Douglas handed over the last piece and jumped down, wiping his sweat away with his fingers.

Within a center square in Noxford County Jail, some inmates were bending, stretching, and working out haphazardly. Douglas was watching. He started a conversation."Good that you guys work out here. Do you want to see how I workout?" He went down on one knee.

A bald, chubby inmate inquired, "And who are you?"

"I am Douglas. I own a gym in the town."

The second inmate interrupted, "Oh sure. What did you do, kill someone, steal something?"

"None of that. I am innocent."

"Everyone says the same thing here. Okay, I am in," the first inmate said.

A few joined in. Lanky and muscular, Douglas led them briefly. The workout was complete.

"Thank you, gentlemen. Good workout. You may sit down," Douglas said.

Everybody settled down on the floor.

"That was good. Now say something," The third inmate said.

"Here comes the speech, "The first inmate commented.

"Let me hear it, man," The third inmate said.

"Folks, what do you learn from life?" Douglas began. "Repentance, forgiveness, new motivation. You have only one life. The past is gone. The past is behind us. The past is dead. Nobody wants to vacation here. One mistake and boom you are here. But the truth always comes out in the end. When the sun slowly rises to the new heights, spreading its bright light, the new dawn begins."

After saying that, Douglas stopped and looked around to see if they liked it or not.

"Go on. Go on," The third Inmate signaled.

"Life is short. The holy book says dry bread is better than stolen cake. Honesty gives rewards."

"Baloney. Then why are we here?" The first inmate said.

The second inmate agreed. "Yeah."

"We have better things to do. Enjoy life for what it is meant for. May be this is God's calling," Douglas kept on going.

The first inmate felt surprised. "Really?"

Douglas concluded, "This may be a God-given transition. You have to make a right turn at the intersection and follow through. The harder the job, the sweeter the reward, they say."

"Right on, preacher man," the second inmate agreed.

"Don't let anyone label you with anything. It is only up to you. Help is there. Douglas paused, clasping both hands together.

He added, "It applies to me first. Next month is my hearing. I am innocent, but I don't have any evidence. Pray for me. Pray for us."

The second inmate started clapping. "Man that was good."

"Thank you, skinny preacher man. I know you are innocent."

And the bell rang. They all got up and dispersed. Some walked to the kitchen, thinking about what Douglas had said. They watched the food being made and chitchatted.

Inmates had gathered near the jail kitchen. It was lunchtime. A stocky jailor in his crisp, ironed uniform arrived with awe. He walked up to Douglas.

"Hey, new fellow, you look nice. What did you do, run out of money?" He displayed a loud, ugly laugh. "Rob a bank? Kill someone?"

Douglas politely replied, "Yes, Officer, I am new. But I did none of the above. I am innocent, just like each one here thinks. It is a fact."

A few guys joined in the conversation with the jail officer.

An inmate said, "You know, Officer, it is getting boring here."

"So, why did you come here in the first place?" the officer yelled at him.

Douglas interrupted to say, "Well, Officer, I have to ask you, is it possible for me to teach a few classical exercises to all the inmates?"

"Yeah, good idea. It will be fun." All the inmates agreed.

"No. They don't care. Don't waste your time."

"Come on! We are all for it," one inmate said.

A few days later, Sheena walked into the prison lobby. A female security guard checked her out. She patted her down. She carried a thick book, a magazine, and a box with her.

The security guard looked at the book. "You can't take this inside, lady. Too heavy, it could become a weapon during a prison brawl."

The officer holds on to the book and gave her a token.

"Ma'am, it is only a holy book of prayer," Sheena requested.

"Whatever. You can't."

"How about this sports magazine?"

"No problem."

Now the security officer pointed at Sheena's box. "And what is this?"

"Ma'am, it is a birthday cake. Today is my brother's birthday," Sheena explained.

"Not allowed."

"Please, please, he will be happy. It is a surprise. You can also taste it." While saying that, Sheena opened the box, removed a candle, took out a plastics knife, cut the cake, and gave her a piece on a paper napkin.

"Some people hide a hacksaw blade like cutters in the cake," said the security officer while munching. She threw away half and walked up to Sheena. With a full mouth, she said, "Go."

Sheena went inside. She sat at the corner table of the visiting room. Relatives and loved ones of other inmates were also waiting to see their kin.

Douglas appeared from behind a screen door. He was dressed in one-piece orange prison overalls. Sheena spotted him and waved. Douglas gave her a dry smile and walked up to her confidently. He hugged Sheena. She cried. Both sat down.

"What happened?" Sheena asked.

"Calm down. How is Mom?"

"She is fine but worried. She trusts you will get out of this soon," Sheena said, wiping her tears away.

"Do you take her to the doctor regularly? She is the only thing I worry about."

"Yes. She does not need any more treatment."

"I am embarrassed. I let you both down," Douglas said.

"You are innocent. You did nothing wrong. What are you going to do now?" Sheena wondered.

Douglas explained the whole thing. "Listen, my hearing is in the first week of next month, and then my fate will be decided."

"Don't worry, Brother. God is with you. The truth will come out."

"But how? These guys are monsters."

"You know I have an idea, if you agree."

"What is it?"

"Remember you helped that government officer on the highway the other day?"

"Which officer?"

"The one whom you drove to the airport and who sent you a thank-you note and a business card, Mr. Maestro or somebody. I will find the card."

"No, no, no. We can't do that, take advantage of a little favor. It is immoral."

"Brother, this is the time."

$ $ $

After returning home, Sheena found what she wanted, Mr. Maestro's card.

The following day, Sheena ventured to Mr. Maestro's office.

A busy, elderly blond-haired gentleman noticed Sheena. "May I help you?" he asked.

"Sir, my name is Sheena. I am Douglas's sister. You know he was taken to jail?"

"Oh, that tea cheater guy?"

"Sir, he is not a cheat. He is innocent. That's why I have a question for you."

"Why me? Who gave you my name?" Maestro wondered.

"Sir, he is the one who once gave you a ride to the airport on the highway. You gave him this card. I am his baby sister."

"Look, I am not a lawyer. Now tell me what I can do for you."

"Sir, Douglas told me not to bother you; even then, I have come here. All I need is your advice."

Sheena showed him a newspaper headline and told him next month was the hearing. She pleaded for help.

Maestro got up and walked back and forth thinking. Suddenly he turned around and sat down.

"Okay, I'll see what I can do. But no guarantees," He told Sheena.

"Thank you, sir. All we need is a little guidance."

The man got up again, walked over to a shelf, pulled out a box, and picked out a business card. He passed the card to Sheena. She read both sides: "Gosford, Davey, and Friedrich Attorneys. Criminal Law. 213-555-9472."

"My friend Gosford is the best attorney in town. Tell him Maestro has sent you and not to charge. He gets free publicity," Maestro explained.

Sheena nodded in agreement and left. After reaching home, Sheena made a few calls. She also explained the plan to her kin.

The next morning, Sheena and Smithy went about searching for this firm. Finally, they arrived at Gosford, Davey, and Friedrich's office. Sheena spoke to the receptionist through a glass window. She waved them inside the office. A dapper, middle-aged bearded guy looked at Sheena.

"So, you are the one who called me on the phone. Come in. Sit down. What can I do for you?" Gosford inquired. He pointed at Smithy. "And who is he?"

"My fiancé, Smithy, sir."

"How can I help you?"

"Mr. Maestro gave me your card. We badly need your help. You may have heard about my brother, Douglas, who was arrested."

"Oh, that crook who stole the recipe."

"No, no, no, sir. He did not steal or copy any recipe. This is why I am here."

"Do you have any proof?"

"No, sir, that's the problem."

"Then I can't help you."

"Sir, I know in my heart my brother is innocent."

"Lady, testimony of the heart is not accepted in a court of law." Gosford paused. "Give me the proof. Okay?"

Sad, Sheena stepped out. Smithy followed.

At home, the aging Rubina was praying in the corner near God's picture. Next to her was a shelf containing religious books.

Sheena dressed in a jumpsuit, walked up to a shelf, picked up an old diary, and went to the phone. She looked in that diary, turned pages, and dialed the phone.

"Hello. Hello … Is this the Din home? I am Sheena from the US. Is Grandma there?"

"Wrong number. Who is this?" Someone picked up the phone.

"Uncle Paul, please wait. This is Sheena, Kamal's daughter. It is very important. May I talk to Grandma?"

"So now you are calling. She is in the Highberg New Life Nursing Home. I don't have her number. Ask the directory," Paul said.

When her uncle hung up, Sheena dialed again.

"Oh yeah, hi, nursing home. My name is Sheena from the US. Is it possible to speak to my grandma Jane, please?"

She waited a while and heard, "Ayllo?"

"Grandma Jane, this is Sheena speaking. How are you?"

"Is this my little baby doll Sheena?" Grandma sobbed.

Sheena got emotional. There was no answer. She waited a while.

"Grandma, do you have that recipe book you used to teach us cooking from when we were young?" Sheena was choking.

"Heh? Which book are you talking about? I don't know. I left everything in the attic. No idea what happened to it."

A big pause.

"But it is very important, Grandma. Have someone look up and send it to us by FedEx please. We badly need it."

"How is my little Dougy?"

"Good. Very good. He will be all right. Bye."

"What? But why? Why?"

"I will tell you later," Sheena assured her.

CHAPTER 10

TRIALS

The Tea Trading Association versus Slim Doug Enterprise trial began. The news media was already waiting on the sidewalk of the courthouse. A large crowd of people was laughing and joking. A police van brought in Douglas. People started pushing and shoving to see him.

People were shouting at him.

"Here comes the big-shot businessman."

"Hey, did you cheat?"

"Who did you steal recipe from?"

"How did you break in? Ha, ha, ha."

The media followed him.

A lady reporter ran after Douglas. Holding her mic out, she asked him, "Mr. Douglas, did you do it? What are you going to say?"

The crowd tried to follow him from behind the barricades.

A guy taunted, "If you drink his tea, you become slim like him."

Second guy said, "Hey, stop drinking beer, you beer bellies."

Douglas was taken inside the courtroom. The bailiff made an announcement.

"Order ... order. Judge Norman Smith presiding. All rise."

An elderly blond judge presided.

MADHU SOLANKI

People stood up. Rubina, Sheena, and Smithy were in the front row. Douglas's faithful employees Jack, Mark, Elijah, and Sandy were also present to support the boss. Moderately dressed, Emily too stood up in a corner, carrying her purse.

Suited and booted, the intimidating plaintiff's party was sitting in front.

The bailiff announced, "Court in session. Case number 9472 Tropical Tea Traders Association versus Douglas Din of SDE Corporation."

The court clerk gave Douglas the Bible.

"Repeat after me. I shall tell the truth, the whole truth, and nothing but the truth."

Douglas agreed, "I will."

"Who is plaintiff's counsel?" Judge Smith asked.

Plaintiff's Attorney Brown stood up.

"It is I, Danny Brown, Your Honor, from Solomon, Schwartz, Johnson and Lowe Associates."

"And from the defendant's side?" Judge Smith asked.

"My name is Jim Gosford, Your Honor. I am volunteering to represent the defendant Douglas Din for free."

"Why free?"

"Doing good work for someone never goes to waste."

"Skip the chitchat. Let's begin. Plaintiff's counsel, who represents on your plaintiff's behalf?"

"Ms. Margie Walters, the tea-trading association secretary."

"What's your complaint?"

"Judge, my client complains that the defendant has maliciously stolen their recipe. Their businesses are suffering," Danny Brown said.

"You may examine the defendant," Judge Smith said.

"So, Mr. Douglas, tell me, how did you obtain the original recipe? When did you break in?"

The defense attorney quickly stood up.

"Objection, Your Honor," Defense Attorney Gosford requested.

"Sustained. You cannot ask direct accusatory questions."

"Your Honor, I am only trying to save time."

He looked at Douglas. "So, Mr. Douglas, tell me about the recipe," the plaintiff's attorney said.

Douglas answered, "What recipe? I don't know what you are talking about. I want to simply focus on my business."

The attorney turned to the judge and said, "Your Honor, the defendant is trying to be cute. He is evading my questions."

"Defendant Douglas, I am informed that you are a model inmate. However, you must answer questions properly," The judge warned Douglas.

"I am sorry, Your Honor."

"You may be innocent, but in the court of law, you have to prove it. The burden of proof is entirely on your shoulders," The judge added. "Mr. Gosford, go," he asked the counsel.

"Honorable Judge, my client is innocent. He should be set free right away. There is no case," he said.

"Mr. Brown?" The judge asked.

Danny Brown continued with Douglas. "Have you ever heard the word *copyright*?"

"Of course, Counsel."

"Then this is a pure copyright infringement. A gross offense. Stealing trade secrets is a serious felony crime."

"The recipe in question is my grandma's original recipe. I modified it by trial and error," Douglas clarified.

People start murmuring. Some agreed, and some showed surprise.

Judge Smith inquired, "Plaintiff's representative, Ms. Margie, do you have any evidence of stealing?"

"Your Honor, his product almost tastes like ours. Everybody says so," Margie answered.

The audience murmured in disagreement.

"Quiet. Who is 'everybody'?" The judge questioned.

"Our customers tell us that the new guy's tea tastes almost like ours. Some say it is even better. Isn't it obvious?"

"Hearsay."

The judge looked at Douglas.

"Defendant, what is your defense? Plaintiff says your tea is better."

"Your Honor better is not right. It is the best tea. Inside, we have custom-grown secret ingredients grown on a tropical mountain, which gives a zing to our product."

Douglas showed him a picture of a beautiful tea garden and continued, "It is grown after making a number of trials using the best homegrown fertilizer."

"Was your recipe copyrighted? What's the copyright number? Was it patented? Name your ingredients," the judge asked Margie.

"Uh … um … I don't know. Maybe they have changed the name. They are a mixture of herbs and spices. And they are proprietary."

"Do you have any proof? Any piece of evidence of stealing or copying? Like a picture, a document, a phone record, or a credible witness?"

Margie replied, "Maybe the defendant broke into one of our shops at night or bribed our employees."

"It is just an assumption, not proof," the judge said.

"Sometimes he used to come to our shops and carry out our products. Perhaps he got them analyzed in a testing lab," Margie said. She added, "Oh yes, when his newly purchased shop was being remodeled, he used to come to our shops, buy our product, and go back to sit on the stool, pretending to supervise workers and enjoy and test our tea."

"What do you mean?" Judge Smith asked.

"He took away our samples. He must have gotten them analyzed in some research lab," Margie said.

"Mr. Defense Counsel, what's your say?"

Mr. Gosford stood up. "If each one of their accusations is like a tiny frog, then their entire narrative becomes a swamp full of squeaking tadpoles."

Judge Smith turned to the defendant. "Mr. Din, the burden of proof is on your shoulders. The book says if you have no defense, then you are guilty. Punishment could be as high as five years."

"I don't know what more to say, Your Honor," Douglas responded.

"Then tell the court how you make your products."

"All I recall is a long time ago, our grandma showed us cooking tricks."

"Oh, now Grandma, who is this grandma? Is she here?" The judge exclaims.

"No. She used to live in the old country. However, I can say that we have done a lot of research. We went to the library, read books, and experimented."

"How do we know?"

"The librarian, Mrs. Edith Kruzakowski, is here."

"Mrs. Edith, come to the witness stand," the bailiff announced.

The gray-haired, middle-aged Edith walked up to the witness stand. She took the oath.

At the same moment, the defense attorney sneaked out of the courtroom, listening to his cell phone.

"So, Mrs. Edith, did you ever see this man?" The defense attorney asked.

"Mr. Din and his sister used to come to the library for recipe books since they were younger," she answered.

"That does not prove anything. You may sit down," the judge said and looked at Mr. Brown. "Counsel, you may continue."

"Honorable Judge, I would like to conclude they have no recipe, no grandma. The defendant is trying to hide the facts. He is guilty. He is a thief," Counsel Brown concluded.

Judge Smith asked Douglas, "Tell me about your grandma. Where is your grandma, the recipe owner?"

"She lives in the old country. She is very old by now."

"That's it? What else do you want to say?"

"Your Honor, again, my straight and honest answer is that I didn't copy, steal, or conspire in my recipe. I am innocent, totally innocent. That's all I can say."

"This is not a defense. I am sorry I have to decide on this side or that. Understand?" The judge looked around. "Again, where is your defense attorney?" Judge Smith shouted. "Where did he go?"

The entire courtroom became dead quiet. An air of uncertainty prevailed on people's faces. They looked around, wondering what would happen next.

Suddenly, the door squeaked open. People turned their heads. Defense Attorney Gosford dashed in announcing, "Wait, Your Honor! Please wait."

He kept running toward the front.

A frail old lady was following behind him. Sheena led her fragile grandma, holding her by the armpit. She was stooping. The lady could hardly walk. She was holding a cane in her left hand and a torn piece of paper in her right hand.

She looked around in amazement. Smithy, Sheena's fiancé, followed them. Douglas turned his head around and watched in surprise. He realized who it was.

"Grandma?"

Grandma looked at Douglas. She lunged toward him.

"Dougy, my baby!"

"Please be quiet," the judge said.

Quickly, Sheena quieted her grandma by putting a finger over her lips.

Plaintiff's Attorney Brown said, "What is this? Some kind of a joke? Nonsense."

People started murmuring.

"Order, order!" Judge Smith used his gavel.

"Pardon us, Judge. Here is the proof you wanted. She is our witness. The grandma. Best proof you can ever have," Defense Attorney Gosford said.

"Have the oath taken," the judge told the bailiff.

The bailiff handed a Bible to grandma. The courtroom clerk administered the oath.

Sheena prompted, "Say yes."

"Yes, yes," her grandma said.

"You may proceed," the judge told the plaintiff's attorney Danny Brown.

"What is this? Who are you?" The plaintiff's attorney asked.

"Huh?" Grandma put her hand on her ears, looking at Sheena.

"What is your name?" Another question.

Sheena started whispering in her ear.

"Uh … Jane," Grandma said.

"How are you related to the defendant?"

Sheena whispered again.

"He my baby. Small baby." She gestured with her hand. She showed his height when he was a baby.

"What have you brought today?" The plaintiff's attorney asked.

"Huh?" Again, Grandma put her hand on her ear.

Sheena instructed her. Grandma reached out to the attorney to give him a piece of worn-out paper and said, "Recipe. Sorry is no whole. Mr. Judge, I come far, far away. Please do something."

The attorney grabbed the old paper containing three punch holes from her hand. It was a handwritten, dirty, torn page without corners. He put on his glasses and read. Immediately, his face became pale. Reluctantly, he passed it to the judge.

The judge looked through his reading glasses and read the compilation of partially legible ingredient names with their quantity and series of steps.

"But, Judge, people say—" the plaintiff's attorney interrupted.

"That's hearsay." The judge stood up and announced, "Court is in recess. A decision will be given right after the break."

As soon as the recess was over, people come into the courtroom and quickly took their seats. Some were talking, murmuring, and wondering what would happen next.

"All rise," the bailiff said.

The judge walked in and took his chair. The bailiff made the announcement.

"Case number 9472 Tropical Tea Traders Association versus Douglas Din of SD Enterprise reconvening."

There was pin-drop silence. Judge Smith cleared his throat and started speaking.

"There is no real proof given by the accuser. All imagination. Sheer fabrication. It appears a bunch of wealthy tycoons are simply harassing a small business. This little piece of paper proves in favor of the defendant. I find the defendant Douglas Din not guilty. Case dismissed. Douglas is acquitted."

People were clapping. There was a big uproar in the crowd. The judge knocked the gavel on the table.

"Order. Order!" the judge commanded, looking around to stop the chaos. "Mr. Douglas, what's your counter claim?"

"Nothing, Your Honor. I don't want any money." Douglas pondered a beat and said, "All I want is justice."

People started murmuring.

"Every good deed has a price to pay. Either monetary or by time or by pain and suffering," the judge said, looking over his reading glasses. "Defendant is awarded five million dollars for a false accusation, wasting his time, and ruining his reputation."

While saying that, the judge nodded at Defense Attorney Gosford. He stood up.

Gosford addressed Douglas, "Don't say no. The flight has arrived just in time. The seat is in first class. Jump in. Fly far, far away. I know you will."

A huge excitement prevailed. Most people walked out smiling.

CHAPTER 11
DESTINATION

Now free, Douglas couldn't wait to get into action. Raw material was coming into a busy Slim Doug Enterprise outfit. The factory department was busy receiving boxes. Machines cleaned and separated the raw material.

On other end, the shipping department looked busy. There was an ad on TV selling Douglas's tea.

A sign on a building was advertised the popular SD Tea University.

The university campus boasted plants in the garden and big theaters inside with research charts. Labs were equipped with Petri dishes, microscopes, pots, burettes, pipettes, and beakers. Some beakers had pinkish brown tea samples. Busy students were dressed in their white lab coats.

Enthusiastic students experimented with hybrid tea plant products like rose plant, cinnamon, and the like, planted in two separate pots.

Over in the cafeteria, there were an all-you-can-drink juice bar and an unlimited buffet, along with coffee, tea, and blended beverages.

Confident, Douglas also got into philanthropic work. Mr. Douglas was invited to speak at the Human Help Institute. He was dressed in a steel-gray suit as he entered the institute along with his entourage. Signs on the door indicated locations of various departments. He walked into a hall filled with workers.

This day, he would be honored by the Human Help Institute's Handicap Laboratory, Vision Research, and Hearing Aid Research and the Feed the Hungry Mission.

A short, chubby, middle-aged director in a brown checkered suit led him through a handicap workshop where artificial limbs were made. They ended up in an assembly hall. The meeting proceeded.

"Ladies and gentlemen, I introduce to you Mr. Douglas Din," the director of the institute greeted the crowd.

Douglas replied in turn, "Folks, I am very happy to be with you today. I am impressed with the notable work you are doing. I am forwarding a donation of a million dollars to your organization. I thank you for your kind service."

His speech ended to huge applause.

Next, they went to a Braille class where students were studying to write in Braille. Douglas went up to a few and touched their shoulders to say hello. Next they passed by a hearing device research lab and finally arrived at a huge room where signs were being made. There was a big sign that read, "Feed the Hungry," being prepared. Douglas shook hands with the organizer and exited. He returned home satisfied.

In the evening, Douglas was sitting on the sofa at home with his papers and the portfolio. Sheena came to Douglas smiling and showed him a few colorful wedding cards.

"Five hundred wedding invitations are ready. I showed it to Mom and Emily, and they liked it very much," Sheena said, showing him a few. "All are looking forward to your great wedding day, Bro!" Sheena mentioned and left the room.

On their wedding day, the proud and radiant newlyweds, Douglas and Emily, came out of the church. People were standing in the street to watch the newly married. And lo, here they came. People applauded. Some gave them a happy shout-out and whistle.

They stepped all the way out in front of the church sidewalk. The paparazzi ran to take pictures. Invited guests greeted the newlyweds.

Douglas's company staff, along with Maestro and Gosford, was present in the crowd. The Indian chief was present in his native garb.

Douglas's business representatives received and greeted the guests. Smithy and Fat Bobby played a big part.

Douglas got super busy after his wedding.

$ $ $

The clock showed 9:00a.m. Within the Wall Street Stock exchange. People were talking inside an office. A gentleman dressed in his jacket and a tie came in and addressed his colleagues.

"Heads up, this is a big day. Today, SD Enterprise is going public."

In the central mall, a guy dressed in a work jacket was preparing fellow workers.

"Guys, it is going to be a big Douglas day today."

Moments later, a limo arrived in front of One Wall Street in the canyons of downtown Manhattan. Douglas and Sheena were being escorted out by a representative.

Brother and sister stepped inside a towering financial exchange building. They walked past a bald, chubby security guard. He saluted them.

They were taken to the central mall near a big board where the bell was located.

An agent announced, "Our new entrepreneurs, Mr. Douglas Din and Ms. Sheena Din, are with us today. We wish them good luck. Good Luck, SDE Corporation."

The staff clapped.

The clapping stopped. Just a couple of minutes before 9:30a.m., the agent whispered some instructions in their ears. Douglas and Sheena rang the opening bell. The market was now open for business. People got on the phones. Agents were running around. The big board became busy. SDE stocks sold like hotcakes. The TV was on inside the Wall Street office.

A TV anchorman said, "Since all stocks have been sold out, expectations are even higher for tomorrow. They may double in value."

The wall TV picture showed the excitement in the street. Crowds of people pushed and shoved to get their copy. Newspaper stalls sold out all their copies.

The anchorman described, "Mr. Douglas Din keeps on opening his new tea stalls and health spas. He has created a franchise. His tropical tea garden is also flourishing."

Country of Prosperia

Douglas visited his old country by a special invitation.

An SDE Airline private jet touched down at Prosperia Airport. A sign on top of the building said, "Welcome to Luckville, Prosperia." Douglas disembarked along with some Slim Douglas Enterprise employees. They got into a shiny black limo, which then drove away.

Arriving cars filled the parking lot of the TV studio. Well-dressed people came out and walked toward the building. It was a festival-like atmosphere.

A huge big banner displayed, "Welcome to Mr. and Mrs. Din's Honor Ceremony. Long Live Douglas Din."

The preshow entertainment was going on inside. After the children had finished singing, dancing, and performing, the audience gave a hearty *applause*. The moderator walked to the mic.

"Thank you all for being here. We are glad to have our great philanthropist Douglas Din with us today. This is where, a few years ago, his late father, Mr. Kamal Din, won Five million dollars in a contest."

The moderator walked toward the front of stage and said, "I request Mr. and Mrs. Din to please come forward."

After they were called, a tanned, tall, confident-looking handsome young man and his new wife, Emily, walked forward and took seats facing people among their great applause. A couple of local children came forward and gave them the flowers and bouquet.

The moderator declared, "We are honored to present the world's best humanitarian award to Mr. Douglas Din."

Douglas got up and gracefully received his trophy for his philanthropy. The hall roared with applause.

Right after the ceremony, a busy Douglas and his entourage stepped into the corporate jet at Luckville Airport. They took their seats, and the plane took off. Douglas settled comfortably in his cushioned seat. He took out a white hanky from his breast pocket and wiped his face. He glanced at the newspapers and magazines set out on a small table. He picked up *My Monetary Matters* magazine. The cover bore the headline "World's New Billionaires."

Douglas opened it and turned the pages. He saw his picture and read the list of new billionaires. "Douglas Din, CEO SDE Corporation," he read somewhere in the middle.

He smiled and shut it. Slowly, he tossed it back on the coffee table.

Back Home

The next morning, the SDE Corporation manager walked to and fro, eagerly staring at the wall clock showing it was past 9:30 a.m. The manager quickly picked up a desk phone.

"Mrs. Din, hello. Is Mr. Din coming to work today? We are waiting for him. He always comes before time."

Emily picked up the phone. "What? He already left early in the morning. Hasn't he arrived yet? My God."

Emily put phone down and quickly dialed Rubina. "Mom, did Dougy come by your side? He did not reach the office yet. Somebody called."

Upset, Rubina asked, "What? Why? How?"

There was a dead silence. She said, "Ah, Sheena also left very early today without telling me. You know what? Today is their father's anniversary. Maybe they are up to something mysterious. Call the police."

The police station tried to get more information from the TV network.

An anchorman in Gowalia TV station said, "Breaking news. Town's rising billionaire Douglas Din is missing. He was supposed to go to his office, but he never arrived. The police department adds that a town hardware store noticed a couple in a limousine buying some garden tools early this morning. Also, a downtown flower lady sold baskets full of expensive flowers to a young couple early this morning."

A picture of the subdued Gowalia Police Department building appeared on the TV.

The anchorman continued, "The Gowalia Police Department has alerted all important checkpoints of the state, especially in the city of Los Angeles."

At Douglas's office, restless SDE staff had gathered together in the manager's office to watch the latest TV news.

At his mother's place, the ailing Rubina was watching her TV with both her hands holding her cane in her living room. She appeared wearing long socks and a heavy, wrinkled robe.

Emily was also watching her kitchen TV, while holding a phone over her ear.

The police department, news media, and a curious crowd of people were eagerly waiting to receive them outside the LA North Side Cemetery gate. A police officer was listening to his high-pitched radio.

"Gowalia PD says they have been missing since morning. Keep an eye out near the cemetery. Today is their dad's death anniversary."

"Copy, Chief."

Everyone was staring inside the North Side Cemetery while keeping eyes on both sides of the road.

People who knew him reminisced about Kamal Din's funeral years before when those two lonely kids ran back to the grave. They had stood together and then knelt, mumbled something, got up, and turned around. They were young Douglas and Sheena. They both ran back.

A buzzing noise was coming closer from the sky. An SDE Corporation helicopter landed in the corner. Two well-dressed individuals removed their noise-reducing devises from their heads and stepped out.

The lady had flowers in her hands. The man carried a broom and some garden tools, including a hand shovel. They walked to Kamal's grave and swept it clean. Kamal's name came out clear. They lit incense sticks and put flowers on the gravestone.

Both Douglas and Sheena stepped back, knelt down, and stayed quiet, making prayer gestures. Then they stood up, raised their hands together, and loudly proclaimed, "Yay, we did it, Dad!"

Grown-up Douglas and Sheena then both turned around with broad smiles.

That's the story of our skinny little boy named Douglas—Slim Douglas the Billionaire—and his little sister, Sheena.

ABOUT THE AUTHOR

 Madhu Solanki came to America in 1971, after obtaining his postgraduate degree in chemical research. He has worked with various chemical companies, eventually retiring from Merck/Schering Plough Institute after working as an Information Scientist.

He speaks four languages and considers English to be his second language. He belonged to Toastmasters International. After retirement he decided to write in order to share his life experience with young generation. He has written books in English with some translated into Asian languages. He has recently finished his fourth screenplay. This story was transpired from one of his screenplays. Details can be acquired from: fourscreenplays@yahoo.com.

Printed in the United States
by Baker & Taylor Publisher Services